SECRETS
OF THE SEVEN

The EAGLE'S QUILL

Also by Sarah L. Thomson

Secrets of the Seven: The Eureka Key

SECRETS
OF THE SEVEN

The EAGLE'S QUILL

SARAH L. THOMSON

BLOOMSBURY
NEW YORK LONDON OXFORD NEW DELHI SYDNEY

First published in the United States of America in April 2017
by Bloomsbury Children's Books
www.bloomsbury.com

Bloomsbury is a registered trademark of Bloomsbury Publishing Plc

For information about permission to reproduce selections from this book, write to
Permissions, Bloomsbury Children's Books, 1385 Broadway, New York, New York 10018
Bloomsbury books may be purchased for business or promotional use. For information
on bulk purchases please contact Macmillan Corporate and Premium Sales Department
at specialmarkets@macmillan.com

Library of Congress Cataloging-in-Publication Data
Names: Thomson, Sarah L., author.
Title: The Eagle's Quill / by Sarah L. Thomson.
Description: New York : Bloomsbury, 2017. |
Series: Secrets of the seven Summary: In Glacier National Park,
middle school geniuses Sam, Martina, and Theo follow clues related to
Thomas Jefferson as they tackle a new round of puzzles, riddles, and traps to
find the next key left behind by the Founding Fathers, but Gideon Arnold,
descendant of the infamous Benedict Arnold, is hot on their trail.
Identifiers: LCCN 2016023141 (print) • LCCN 2016049666 (e-book)
ISBN 978-1-61963-733-7 (hardcover) • ISBN 978-1-61963-734-4 (e-book)
Subjects: | CYAC: Puzzles—Fiction. | Antiquities—Fiction. | Secret societies—Fiction. |
Jefferson, Thomas, 1743–1826—Fiction. | Glacier National Park (Mont.)—Fiction.
Classification: LCC PZ7.T378 Eag 2017 (print) |
LCC PZ7.T378 (e-book) | DDC [Fic]—dc23
LC record available at https://lccn.loc.gov/2016023141

Book design by Colleen Andrews
Typeset by Integra Software Services Pvt. Ltd.
Printed and bound in the U.S.A. by Berryville Graphics Inc., Berryville, Virginia
2 4 6 8 10 9 7 5 3 1

All papers used by Bloomsbury Publishing, Inc., are natural, recyclable products
made from wood grown in well-managed forests. The manufacturing processes
conform to the environmental regulations of the country of origin.

SECRETS
OF THE SEVEN

The EAGLE'S QUILL

To my dear and trusted friend Josiah Hodge, greetings.

My thoughts and hopes will travel westward with you, Captain Lewis, Lieutenant Clark, and the other members of the Corps of Discovery. How I wish I might accompany you, to discover the length and breadth of our land, to encounter tribes unknown to us, and to come face-to-face at last with the distant and mighty Pacific. The trials and difficulties of life here in the President's House seem petty and unimportant compared with the quest that you and your companions are undertaking.

And you, my friend, bear a responsibility that no other member of the expedition can share. With this letter, I entrust the Eagle's Quill to your care. The Quill penned the Declaration that gave our nation its birth; it will now help to protect that nation from enemies within and without. You know that our enemies are many, some even in our own midst.

Keep the Quill safe at all times. When you reach your destination, hide it in a most secret and protected location known only to yourself. Reveal its existence to no one except, as your life nears its end, to one of your own family whom you can trust to carry on the charge. I pray, as do all the Founders, that we will never be called upon to use the secret the Quill protects. But that is for the ages to decide.

Farewell, my friend. In this life, we shall not meet again. But our shared duty to our newborn country will keep our hearts and minds close for as long as our lives last.

> With most sincere esteem
> and regard,
>
> *Thomas Jefferson*

CHAPTER ONE

Sam took another bite of his Snickers bar and chewed slowly, unable to take his eyes from the view outside the helicopter window.

For the past few hours, he'd been watching the flat, dry, dusty landscape of Nevada sort of crumple and heave itself upward, first into gentle green hills, then into taller slopes. After a stop to refuel, they had finally reached Montana, where towering peaks stabbed up through pine forests into a sky that was so blue it practically glowed.

Sam had never seen mountains this big before. This steep. This . . . this . . . *mountainy*. The sheer size of it all was making his brain reel. He could almost hear a soundtrack playing in the distance: "O beautiful, for spacious skies, for amber waves of grain. For purple mountain majesties . . ."

And to make things even better, nobody was trying to kill him or any of his friends. Right this minute, anyway. Lately Sam had learned not to take that kind of thing for granted.

The person sitting next to Sam poked him with a finger. Sam turned to glance at Martina—Marty—Wright. Her eyes were lit up with excitement behind her glasses, and her black hair, chopped off at the level of her chin in a line so straight you could use it for a ruler, swung beneath her headset. Under a fleece jacket she wore a purple T-shirt that said THE PAST, THE PRESENT, AND THE FUTURE WALKED INTO A BAR. IT WAS TENSE.

"Did you know that Glacier National Park was the tenth national park to be established?" Marty asked. She was speaking into the headset; Sam wore a similar one. The noise from the helicopter rotors was so loud that without the headsets on you couldn't hear a word anybody said.

"Nope," Sam said. He didn't add that he didn't care much either. Marty knew a lot of stuff, and she liked to share it. Sometimes it could be irritating, but there had been times in the past few days when the things Marty knew had saved Sam's life.

Still, that didn't mean he had to listen to her twenty-four/seven, did it?

"And did you know—" she started to say.

"So, listen," he interrupted her. "What do you think we're going to be looking for when we land? Got any ideas about what our old pal Ben Franklin would have wanted us to find in Montana?"

"Do tell us some more about Glacier National Park, Ms. Wright," cut in a cool voice, one that belonged to Evangeline Temple. She was seated across from Marty, and when Sam glanced at her, she skewered him with her gaze and nodded toward the helicopter pilot. Obviously she wanted Sam to stop talking into his headset when the guy could hear.

"Well, it has one of the largest remaining grizzly bear populations in the lower forty-eight states," Marty said with enthusiasm. "Did you know that some scientists consider polar bears to be a subspecies of grizzly bears? And how about this . . ."

Sam scratched behind his left ear, and while his hand was up there, pressed the button that turned his headset from *on* to *off*. Marty's voice went silent, although her mouth kept moving. Sam smiled and nodded, wide-eyed and eager, which seemed to make Marty happy. She kept on moving her mouth as Sam turned his face back to the window.

This time, however, he focused his gaze not on the landscape whizzing past, but on the faint reflection he could see of Evangeline and the person next to her.

Tall and slim, her dark hair streaked with white and very smooth under her headset, Evangeline seemed to be listening to Marty, but it was hard to tell. For all Sam knew, she'd switched off her headset just as he had, and she was busy daydreaming about Betsy Ross singing a karaoke version of "Yankee Doodle" with some steel drums for backup.

Next to her, Theo—Theodore Washington—slouched in a seat that looked too small for him. But everything looked too small for Theo. He made the whole helicopter seem like something from a kid's G.I. Joe collection.

Theo was staring out of the window just as Sam had been, without a word to say. That wasn't unusual. Sam had known Theo only a few days, and the one thing he knew for sure about the big guy was that Theo didn't speak up unless it was to say something that mattered.

As Sam watched, Theo frowned, and his fingers began to tap out a restless rhythm on the armrest of his seat. And for some reason that Sam couldn't quite put his finger on, Theo didn't look like a guy who was staying quiet because he didn't have anything to say. Instead he looked like a guy who had plenty to say but wasn't saying any of it.

Weird. But then everything had been weird for days now, when it hadn't been terrifying, astonishing, or just plain impossible to believe.

And life didn't show signs of getting back to normal anytime soon.

Sam kept watching the two faces, Evangeline's pale ivory and Theo's dark brown, both superimposed on a rushing landscape of conifers and rocky peaks and cloud-swept sky. He really wished he knew a bit more about the things Theo wasn't saying. Evangeline too. The pair of them had not always been exactly up front about what they knew and what they were planning.

In fact, there were times when they had straight-out lied.

Evangeline had pretended to be running a puzzle contest, the kind of thing Sam loved to enter. The American Dream Contest. Sam had been so excited when he'd gotten that letter in the silver envelope, the one that said he'd won. His prize? The trip of a lifetime.

Well, Evangeline sure hadn't lied about that part.

What she hadn't told him—not at first, anyway—was that this trip of a lifetime would involve a crazy trek across the entire country, trying to find seven artifacts hidden in seven secret locations. Those artifacts were the key to finding some bizarre super-weapon from way back in Revolutionary War times, something Ben Franklin himself had invented. That's what Evangeline claimed, anyway.

Sam dug around in his pockets and fished out a crumpled receipt and a chewed-up ballpoint pen. He smoothed the receipt on his knee and wrote, *Any idea what kind of*

weapon Ben F. would dream up? Death ray? Nuclear bomb?
Photon torpedo?

He passed the note to Marty. She looked down at it and frowned, shook her head, snatched the pen from his hand, and wrote until she ran out of receipt.

She handed the note back. *Really, Sam? Nobody in Revolutionary Days even knew what an atom was. How could Ben Franklin come up with—*

Marty found a little notebook in the inside pocket of her jacket. She flipped it open and finished what she had been writing.

—a nuclear weapon?

Sam took the notebook from her and wrote. *So no bomb. What else could it be? Ideas?*

Insufficient data, Marty wrote back. *For now we have to concentrate on finding the next artifact.*

Sam opened Marty's notebook to a new page. Quickly, he drew a sketch of the picture that had sent them to Montana—a mountain, a goat, a black foot, and a guy with a flat head. It had been Marty who had figured out what the images meant; she was nearly as good at puzzles as Sam was. Nearly.

The mountain and the goat together meant the Rockies, and the body parts stood for the Blackfoot and the Flathead, Native American tribes who lived near Glacier National Park. If Marty was right, and if they were very, very lucky, they should be able to find their second artifact somewhere inside that park.

The things had been hidden—way too well, as far as Sam was concerned—by a secret society called the Founders, descendants of the Founding Fathers themselves. There were two of them right here in this helicopter— Evangeline, a descendant of Benjamin Franklin, and Theo, the several-times great-nephew of George Washington.

The Founders had stashed the artifacts, and then they'd filled their hiding places with puzzles and traps, making sure that only the right people would get their hands on stuff like the key that Benjamin Franklin had flown from his famous kite. The key that, yesterday, Sam had actually held in his hand.

And Evangeline and Theo had not mentioned any of this. Not right away, at least. Sure, they'd come clean now—after everything that had happened in Death Valley, where Sam and Marty and Theo had fallen down flooded mine shafts and solved deadly underground puzzles and nearly been electrocuted—Marty *had* actually been electrocuted!—and escaped scary guys with guns.

But did that mean, Sam wondered, that Evangeline and Theo had told him and Marty about everything? Or did those two have more surprises in store?

Sam shook his head, shoved the notebook back at Marty, lifted the last of his Snickers bar to his mouth, and felt his teeth close on paper. He'd eaten the whole thing, barely tasting it. What a waste. He licked a smear of chocolate off the wrapper just as the helicopter tilted, and his stomach squeezed itself up against the back of his throat. The ground outside his window swooped closer. They were coming in for a landing.

Marty put the notebook back in her pocket, and then she reached toward Sam's head and pressed his headset's *on* button. "So, *like I was saying*"—she zapped a pointed look in his direction—"Lewis and Clark wouldn't have gotten anywhere without Sacagawea. And all she gets is one dinky little dollar coin that won't even go in most vending machines. Totally unfair. And—"

"We'll be hitting the ground in Whitefish in about ten minutes or so," crackled the pilot's voice, cutting off Marty midsentence. He'd probably figured out that waiting for Marty to be done talking was like waiting for the sun to be done shining. It would happen eventually, but could you really hold out for several billion years?

Sam listened to Marty's fifty most fascinating facts about the Lewis and Clark Expedition while the helicopter got lower and lower, finally touching down on a landing strip. Sam was the first one out the door.

It wasn't much of an airport, he thought as he jumped down to the tarmac. A couple of little planes and choppers like theirs were scattered here and there, and one low building was in the distance. He drew in a deep breath of the fresh, cool air and shivered a little. Quite a difference from the blazing heat of Death Valley, where he had woken up this morning.

But it wasn't just the chill in the breeze that made that little hint of uneasiness creep up Sam's spine. One of the many things that Evangeline and Theo had failed to mention early on was that the four of them weren't the only ones trying to get their hands on the Founders' artifacts. They had competition in this race. The other team was headed up by a scary guy named Flintlock, who worked for a man called Gideon Arnold.

Sam remembered Arnold's pale, almost colorless eyes, and the icy way they had looked at Sam and his friends over the barrel of a gun. The guy knew how to hold a grudge, that was for sure. He was still furious about what had happened to his who-knew-how-many-times-great-grandfather, Benedict Arnold himself. America's most infamous traitor. And, more important, Gideon Arnold was ready to kill anybody who got between him and the Founders' artifacts.

Could Arnold be here right now? Watching them? Sam brooded about that while the four of them hauled their suitcases through the airport and Evangeline waved a hand at a taxi waiting by the curb. Could some of Arnold's spies be hanging around in baggage claim? Could the taxi driver be in Arnold's pay? It wasn't impossible. One thing Sam had learned on his little jaunt through Death Valley was not to ever, under any circumstances, underestimate Gideon Arnold.

The taxi swept them along a highway and into the little town of Whitefish. They rolled over a bridge with a shallow river flowing underneath and piled out of the cab when their driver announced that they had made it downtown.

It didn't look like much of a downtown to Sam. No skyscrapers, maybe two traffic lights, about a dozen wooden storefronts lining either side of the street. One sign declared that its building was the WILD, WILDER, WILDEST WEST SALOON!!! With three exclamation marks. Sam counted them. Next door was a store with a wide window full of ten-gallon hats and intricately tooled cowboy boots.

Evangeline paid the cabbie (who didn't seem to be an agent of Gideon Arnold's after all) and asked him where they could find a good outdoor supply store. "We will need to do some shopping," she said as the driver took off. She pointed up the street. Marty headed in that direction, in front of Sam. Evangeline and Theo trailed behind.

"Just look at those mountains," Marty gushed, pointing to the view at the end of the street. She tipped her face up to appreciate the snow-covered slabs of rock, glowing in the amber light of early afternoon. "Quite a change from the desert, right, Sam? Sam?"

"Uh-huh," Sam grunted. Marty was staring around like a tourist, and Evangeline and Theo were muttering together, so it looked like it was up to Sam to keep an eye out for the bad guys. Trouble was, he didn't know exactly what he was looking for. It wasn't like Arnold's employees wore little name tags announcing, "Hi! My name is Bob, and I work for a homicidal maniac!"

Anyway, every other person in this little town seemed somehow out of place to Sam's eyes. It was because most of the people walking by were tourists, he realized. They wore hiking boots and fleece jackets and multipocketed fishermen's vests, and they were consulting maps or guidebooks or looking around like Marty, marveling at the scenery.

Sam followed Marty down the sidewalk, passing a drugstore, a gallery full of Native American artifacts, places advertising helicopter tours and white-water rafting, and a bakery selling cinnamon buns that smelled so good Sam nearly forgot he was supposed to be watching out for sinister henchmen.

"We have to—" Sam heard Theo say from behind him, but he didn't finish the sentence.

"We have to *go where the clues take us,*" Evangeline answered, her low voice full of meaning. "No matter how hard it is."

Bang!

Without a second thought, Sam threw himself at Marty, dragging her down behind a car parked by the curb. Heart pounding, he craned his neck, trying to see around a muddy tire to where the gunshots were coming from.

"Sam! Would you get off me now?" Marty said from underneath him. "Ow!"

"Mr. Solomon?" Evangeline's startled voice came from above.

Sam lifted his head. Theo gave him a funny look. Everybody seemed to be giving him funny looks. Tourists had stopped to stare and a little kid in a stroller was giggling madly.

Bang!

Somebody on the far side of the street was laughing—a guy right in front of the Wild, Wilder, Wildest West Saloon, decked out in a cowboy suit complete with a bright-blue hat and boots the size of Texas.

"Sorry I startled you there, pardner!" the guy called out, letting off another burst of explosions from his cap pistol. "Show starts in ten minutes, folks! Don't be late, it'll be great! Right here in the wildest saloon this side of the Mississippi!"

Kids around him shouted and jumped in excitement. One boy in a black T-shirt with a pirate's skull on the back doubled over with laughter, pointing at Sam and Marty.

Sam felt his face heating up. He struggled to get off Marty without squashing her further. She helped by shoving him to one side and getting up herself, while the stupid fake cowboy waved and hooted and ushered a group of tourists into the saloon.

"You're not hurt, Ms. Wright?" Evangeline brushed a bit of sidewalk grit off Marty's jacket while Theo, straight-faced, offered Sam a hand up.

"I'm fine," Marty said, settling her glasses back on her nose. "But Sam—that was a total overreaction. Do we need to get you checked out for post-traumatic stress disorder or something?"

"Give it a rest, Marty," Sam muttered as they kept walking down the sidewalk, with Evangeline and Theo in front this time.

She put a hand on his arm. "Sam? Really. You're okay, right?" she asked, too softly for the other two to hear.

Sam gave her a sideways look. "Just a case of terminal embarrassment," he told her, keeping his tone light, and glad that Marty had no way of guessing how painfully his heart was still hammering inside his rib cage. He sought for a way to change the subject and found one. "Where do you think we'll find the next clue?"

"It could be anywhere." Marty looked around and shook her head. "Well, not anywhere, I suppose. The artifacts were all moved to their present locations around the time of the Civil War, remember?"

"I remember, yeah," Sam answered.

"So maybe we could go to the library and get a map of the town from that era. That could give us some idea of where to start. Or the town historical society, that might be good. Once we dig up some information, we'll—"

"Information, huh?" Sam asked, pointing to a building just ahead. "That looks like a good place to get information. Hey, Theo, Evangeline, how about we take a look in here?"

A sign on the building read GLACIER NATIONAL PARK INFORMATION CENTER. Sam led the way inside. The minute they were through the door, Marty darted away from Sam's side.

"Ooh, guidebooks!" she exclaimed. "And topographical maps!"

Theo and Evangeline moved off into the information center as well. Sam hesitated just inside the door, looking over shelves of protein bars and water bottles and compasses and first-aid kits and lots and lots of books. Hiking guides. Fly-fishing guides. Wildlife guides. Wildflower guides.

Information . . . right. This place was full of information. But what kind did they need, exactly?

Restless, he wandered over to a spinner rack of post-cards and gave it a whirl. He picked out a nice one of mountain peaks against a blue sky to send to his parents. His mom and dad still thought he was on the American Dream tour, visiting major historical sites and solving some puzzles along the way. He'd send them a postcard in a day or two, but there was no way he could tell them what was really going on.

Beside the postcards was a whiteboard with *Weather Report* scrawled across the top. Below was written *"Today: sun and clouds. Tomorrow: sun, turning cloudy in the afternoon. Tomorrow night: heavy rains expected. FLASH FLOOD WARNING!!!!"*

Great, Sam thought. Flash floods, Gideon Arnold, and Marty with a new guidebook. Which would be more deadly?

He dropped the postcard into the pocket of his sweat-shirt. A weather report was not the kind of information they needed right now. He caught sight of Theo across the store, standing with Evangeline in front of a map that reached from floor to ceiling. Well, that seemed like a good place to start.

"Any clues?" he asked Theo when he reached his side.

Theo shrugged. "It's a lot of terrain to cover," he said. "Especially if we don't know exactly what we're looking for. What we need is a place to start."

Sam looked at the map. He took a step back and tipped his head up and looked at it some more. "How big is this park anyway?" he asked.

"Over a million acres," Marty's voice answered. She'd come up behind him, still holding a new guidebook with a finger marking her place, a bunch of brochures in her other hand.

Sam sighed. "So we think there's a clue hidden somewhere in a million acres of park land?"

"Perhaps here, perhaps elsewhere," Evangeline said. "If you and Ms. Wright will take a look, I will see if the rangers can tell us anything." She set off across the store, headed for a pair of rangers in olive-green uniforms. Theo trailed behind her.

"Come on, Sam. Focus." Marty settled her glasses on her nose and leaned forward. "Do you see anything that might be a clue?"

Sam shrugged. "How about that?" he asked, pointing. "Lost Lake. Because I sure am lost."

"Get serious. Oh! Goat Haunt Overlook!"

"What? Goat Haunt? Why would we want to be visited by the spirits of dead goats?"

"The drawing inside Benjamin Franklin's key!" Marty looked around and lowered her voice. She tapped the pocket that held her little notebook and shot Sam a meaningful look. "Remember? The picture of a goat? Maybe that's the clue."

"There was other stuff in that drawing too," Sam said.
"Is there anything here that looks like a foot or a head?"
Usually arguing with Marty helped him think. But this
time, his brain remained stubbornly blank. "Look, there's
the Flathead National Forest."

"But that's not in the actual park."

"Do you think Ben Franklin knew the boundaries of
the actual park? Did it even exist back then?"

"Fine. But see, there's a Goat Lick Overlook too."

"Will you stop blabbering on about goats?" Sam
snapped.

"Will you stop being so negative?" Marty snapped back.

"Can I help you two?" someone asked from behind
them. Sam turned to see a plump, smiling woman in a
ranger's uniform. "Are you looking for a place to hike or
fish? Anything I can recommend?"

"Uh, no thanks," Sam mumbled, and he pulled Marty
a few feet away. "I'm not being negative," he told her in a
low voice as the ranger turned to point out a good fishing
lake to a man in a baseball cap. "There's just no way a giant
map is going to help. We can't search every spot in this park
that mentions a goat or a foot or a—"

"Caractacus!" Marty exclaimed.

Sam frowned. "Isn't that some sort of eye disease?"

Marty looked at him coldly. "Seriously? No—it's a
place!" She seized Sam's arm and dragged him over to a

rack of brochures. "I saw it before, only I didn't realize . . . There!" She seized the shiny slip of paper and waved it in Sam's face. "Theo! Evangeline! Come and look at this! Caractacus Ranch!"

Sam caught a glimpse of several horses on the front of the brochure, along with a grinning family of tourists all wearing cowboy hats. "A ranch? Marty, this isn't a Wild West show. What does a ranch have to do with anything?"

"Caractacus was Thomas Jefferson's favorite horse!" Marty said loudly. Startled tourists glanced at her over the shelves of books and camping supplies. She turned down the volume but kept waving the brochure at Sam, nearly swatting him in the nose, as Theo and Evangeline reached them. "It's a clue. I'm sure it's a clue. Benjamin Franklin must have sent us to find Thomas Jefferson's artifact!"

"Because of a horse's name?" Sam took the brochure to stop Marty from whacking him in the face with it. "That's a little . . . thin, don't you think? I mean, for all we know George Washington had a dog named, I don't know, Spot."

"He didn't," Theo put in, and plucked the brochure from Sam's hand to frown at it.

Sam rolled his eyes. "I'm just saying, pet names? That's what we're chasing after now?"

"It's a better clue than 'Lost Lake,'" said Marty frostily. "But fine. Go ahead. Find something better."

"By all means." Evangeline, in her turn, took the brochure from Theo. "If you find something else, Mr. Solomon, we will have two avenues to pursue. And if not, we will try Ms. Wright's idea."

Sam could not find anything better. He did try. But after flipping through books and brochures and guides and even coming back to stare at the big map until his eyeballs ached, he could not find anything that even resembled the ghost of a hint of a clue.

"Caractacus Ranch it is," Evangeline said. "I hope they have four rooms available."

"I hope they don't expect me to ride a horse," Sam replied. "Or—"

He broke off as a pack of kids burst into the room from the sidewalk outside. One of them was wearing a black T-shirt and waving a gun. Sam jerked back as the kid pointed the pistol right at his chest.

"Bang!" the boy shouted, and pulled the trigger. Water squirted out of the black plastic gun and splattered the front of Sam's sweatshirt. Sam flinched. His elbow knocked over a display of bright silver whistles.

The kid doubled over in laughter. Theo scowled at him. He didn't move; he didn't have to. Theo could look extremely ominous just standing still.

The boy stopped laughing and fled back outside, followed by his friends. Sam could see the pirate skull on the back of his T-shirt.

Theo picked up the display, setting it upright with a jerk and scattering whistles all over the floor. "Get a grip, Sam," he said. "We've still got supplies to pick up. We can't just hang around here all day."

"Yeah, okay, thanks for—" Sam started to say, but Theo was already walking toward the door, hands in his pockets, head down, so that Sam suddenly found himself talking to the big guy's back.

"What's *his* problem?" Sam asked, brushing water off his sweatshirt. Marty shook her head. Evangeline looked thoughtful. All three of them followed Theo out the door. Then Sam had to hurry back inside to pay for his postcard.

Chapter Two

First they shopped. Sam and Theo and Marty had lost their smartphones, their backpacks, and a lot of their belongings when they'd been taken prisoner by Gideon Arnold the day before, and Evangeline, credit card in hand, insisted on replacing what had been taken.

"But this is all so expensive," Marty protested as Evangeline held up a waterproof, insulated jacket to her shoulder to check its size. She already had a new backpack at her feet, stuffed with more outdoor gear than a Girl Scout troop would need for a weeklong trek through the wilderness.

"The Founders do not lack for resources," Evangeline said, and gave her a quick, reassuring smile. It was the friendliest Sam had seen her look so far. Personally, Sam had no trouble spending the Founders' money. He figured if he was going to dodge their traps and solve their puzzles, the least they owed him was a new phone with the latest apps.

It took the rest of the afternoon for Marty to replace all the supplies that she'd lost and pick up several dozen more things that she considered essential. Sam, once he had a new backpack on his back and a new phone in his pocket, decided to leave her to it. He'd seen a shop on a side street that he thought might be worth investigating.

He thought of asking Theo to come with him, but one glance at the boy's face as he sat frowning on a bench, waiting for Marty to finish comparing GPS units, was enough to squash that idea. Theo looked like a guy who seriously wanted to be alone.

So Sam promised to meet them all in twenty minutes, quickly scanned the street for suspicious characters or kids in pirate T-shirts, and spent fifteen of his free minutes in a little store that had a very nice selection of classic comic books and wasn't too shabby in the junk food department. Marty didn't like to venture out into the world without waterproof distress flares and enough protein bars to feed a very hungry army, but Sam had different priorities.

Then they were off to Caractacus Ranch, with Evangeline at the wheel of their rented SUV. It didn't take long to get out of town and for the view out of Sam's window to shift from stores to houses to trees. Theo, up front next to Evangeline, kept his eyes on the map on his phone and gave terse directions.

"You know, Thomas Jefferson was probably the smartest of all the presidents," Marty said cheerfully as they drove. "He wrote the Declaration of Independence. Well, other people helped too. John Adams put in some stuff. But Jefferson did most of the work, and they followed his first draft pretty closely. And he made the Louisiana Purchase when he was president, which doubled the size of the United States."

"Louisiana isn't that big," Sam said.

"Sam, really. Didn't you ever pay attention in history class? The Louisiana Purchase was a lot more than just Louisiana. It included territory up to Canada. Jefferson was an architect too. He designed his plantation, Monticello. Plus he played the violin."

Theo's low voice drifted back from the front seat. "Sure. He was a great guy. For a slave owner."

"Well." Marty hesitated. Sam saw, with surprise, that for once she was not sure how to reply. "That's true. Of course. Some of the Founders—"

"He wrote, 'All men are created equal,'" Theo interrupted. "How could the man who wrote that have kept hundreds of people as slaves? How equal were *they*? What a hypocrite."

"Yeah, that's a good point," Sam put in. Mostly he was just happy to see Marty stuck for a moment, but the more he thought about it, the more he agreed with Theo.

"But, Theo . . . ," Marty began. Theo didn't let her finish.

"He kept *his own children* as slaves. Did you know that?" Evangeline glanced sideways at Theo, a concerned look on her face, then turned her eyes back to the road as he went on. "One of the women he owned, Sally Hemings, he had seven children with her. Four who lived to grow up. And they were slaves in his house."

"But he freed them," Marty said, a little weakly.

"Eventually. Some not until after he died. What a great guy."

Marty got quiet. Which was quite an achievement on Theo's part.

"Jefferson had kids?" Sam asked. He wasn't sure he really wanted a part of this conversation; Theo sounded seriously irritated, Marty looked anxious, and Evangeline didn't seem to be in any mood to interfere. But an idea had popped into his head.

"Two daughters with his wife," Marty answered quietly. "Two who lived to become adults, anyway. And yes, children with Sally Hemings as well."

"Then he's got descendants?" Sam asked. "Like, you know, you guys? I mean, you're not *his* descendants—

Jefferson's—but you are somebody's. I guess everybody is somebody's. But you know what I mean."

"Astonishingly, I do," Evangeline said. "And yes. Thomas Jefferson has living descendants. As do all the Founders."

"So why are we the ones looking for this artifact, whatever it is? Can't one of them find it?"

"One of them could. His name is James Randolph," Evangeline answered. "Unfortunately, he is unavailable at the moment."

"What, did he turn his cell phone off?"

"He is, I believe, leading a trek near Annapurna, Nepal. Where phone service is not the best. He has not responded to any attempts at contact."

"Of course he hasn't." Sam sighed. "So it's up to us?"

"It seems to be. Mr. Solomon, you must understand that, for a great many years, there has been no serious threat to the Founders' artifacts. This has led to some"—she paused, searching for the right word—"complacency. The Founders were not, shall I say, used to taking on an active role in protecting their inheritance. When my father . . ." She took a breath as if to firm up her voice. "When he disappeared, I knew that something was wrong. But as I could not tell the others exactly what danger we faced, I did not find it easy to convince them. It was only when the three of you encountered Gideon Arnold in Death Valley that the peril to all of us, and to the country, became entirely clear." Her hands tightened on the steering wheel. "One of my associates did believe me from the beginning."

Theo clicked his phone off suddenly and turned to stare out the side window.

"She attempted to check on the safety of several of the artifacts," Evangeline went on. "But we have had no word from her in quite a while, I am sorry to say."

"Oh." Sam winced a little. That did not sound good.

"And that is why I started the American Dream competition. The Founders needed allies. I believe we have found them."

Sam had to admit that made him feel sort of good. Allies. Him and Marty, on the side of the good guys.

As long as the good guys were sharing all their information, of course.

"Oh!" Marty said suddenly. "There's a sign—Theo, didn't you see the sign? For Caractacus Ranch. Turn left. Right there! No, I mean left there!"

Evangeline did so, and they bounced up a gravel road, clouds of dust rising under the SUV's wheels.

"Look!" The car rounded a bend, and Marty pointed up ahead. "It's the ranch! Oh yes. This is the right place for sure."

"What are you talking about?" Sam leaned forward to peer between Evangeline and Theo's shoulders. A gravel driveway wound up a smooth green hill and led to a large white house. It didn't look very much like a ranch to Sam. It looked more like something out of *Gone with the Wind*, a mansion with pillars all along a front porch and a dome rising above.

"It looks like Monticello," Marty breathed. "The dome, those columns. It was designed to look like Thomas Jefferson's house!"

"Let us hope you are correct, Ms. Wright." Evangeline brought the SUV to a gentle stop in front of the house. They got out, and Sam took a careful look at the big white building. He began to feel a familiar excitement—the feeling of being one step closer to solving a puzzle—bubble up inside him. He had the sense that Marty had been right. Good old Marty. Their next clue really could be here.

As they stood together by the car, the front door of the house opened and a man came down the steps of the porch. "Hello. Can I help you?" he asked, a cheerful smile on his face. He was as tall as Theo, and his thick brown hair was touched with gray. Cowboy boots on his feet scuffed through the gravel as he walked toward them.

"I certainly hope so," Evangeline said. "Are you the owner of Caractacus Ranch?"

The man nodded. "Charley Hodge, that's me. Were you hoping for a trail ride? I'm afraid we're not going out on

any more rides today. But we can put you on the list for
tomorrow, if that's what you'd like?"

A trail ride! That was about the last thing Sam wanted.
The last time he'd been on a horse, it had been a pony
at his best friend Adam's fourth birthday party, and the
thing had given him an evil look and stepped on his toe.
Since then he'd steered clear of horses. He'd take a dirt
bike any day.

"No thank you," Evangeline said. "Actually, we're
here on . . . business. My name, Mr. Hodge, is Evangeline
Temple." She waited for a moment, as if to see if
the name meant anything to him.

If it did, he didn't show it. Sam glanced over at Marty,
worried. This guy didn't seem like he'd be of any help. Maybe
Marty Always-Wright had been wrong, just this once.

"Pleased to meet you," Charley Hodge said politely,
but he looked kind of baffled. His gaze swept over Sam,
Marty, and Theo, his confusion only increasing. "And these
guys? Your kids, or . . . ?"

As if she couldn't help herself, Evangeline glanced
sideways at Sam. "Ah, no." Was he imagining that slightly
appalled look on her face? She introduced the children
and then slipped off her jacket, handing it to Theo. Underneath it she wore a pale-blue sleeveless dress. "Thank you
for your welcome, Mr. Hodge." She reached forward to
shake his hand.

Sam could spot the tattoo on her upper arm, the pyramid with an open eye above it and a key inside. He knew it was the secret sign of the Founders, and it marked Evangeline as what she was—a direct descendant of Benjamin Franklin.

Charley Hodge shook Evangeline's hand once and then stopped. His eyes went to her arm, then to her face. She nodded.

Theo shrugged off his jacket too and rolled up his sleeve. On the inside of his forearm was his own tattoo—another pyramid, this one with a sword inside.

"I feel kind of underdressed," Sam whispered to Marty, who elbowed him in the ribs.

Mr. Hodge swallowed and looked quickly around, as if checking to make sure they were safe. He lowered his voice to a whisper—despite the fact that there probably wasn't another person within miles of here. "You're Founders? Both of you?" Eyes wide, he looked over at Sam and Marty. "And them?"

"Mr. Solomon and Ms. Wright are our associates." Evangeline was putting on her jacket again and buttoning it up. "Can we speak inside, Mr. Hodge? We have a matter of some urgency to discuss."

Charley Hodge was shaking his head. "I never thought. I never really thought I'd be the one—yes, of course! Inside! Please! Ms. Temple, kids, come on in."

He led them up the steps of the front porch and into Caractacus Ranch.

Sam had thought a ranch would involve something sort of western—furniture hacked out of logs maybe, Navajo blankets, deer heads on the walls. Instead, he felt as if he were walking into the White House. Charley Hodge led them into a many-sided foyer with an intricately inlaid floor, and then into a living room where bookshelves stood along creamy white walls, a crimson rug lay on the floor, and a fire crackled in a fireplace. "Anita! Abby!" Hodge was calling. "Come quickly! There are people here you have to meet!"

Anita turned out to be Mrs. Hodge—as tall as her husband, with neat silver-blond hair tucked into a bun, corduroy pants, and a plaid shirt buttoned to her throat. Abby ran into the room right after Anita, and she looked to be about Sam and Marty's age, with her mom's blond hair and her dad's excited grin. She looked around, bouncing a little on her sneakered feet, eager to hear her dad's news.

After Anita and Abby had both stared, wide-eyed, at Evangeline's and Theo's tattoos (Theo looked embarrassed, Evangeline cool and smiling), they settled down on couches and chairs. Abby and Sam grabbed pillows in front of the fire.

"The responsibility has been passed down for generations," Charley Hodge said, still shaking his head as if he couldn't quite believe it. "My father told me that one day someone with tattoos like yours might show up, and I'd have to do everything I could to help them recover the Quill."

"The Quill?" Evangeline asked quickly.

"That's what my family has been guarding all these years. The Eagle's Quill. The one Thomas Jefferson used to write the first draft of the Declaration of Independence."

"Told you!" Marty mouthed at Sam, with a self-satisfied smirk on her face. Sam rolled his eyes. As he did so, he caught Abby's gaze on him. A quick smile spread across her face, and he couldn't help smiling back. Then Abby wiped the grin away and turned back to her father, straight-faced. Sam felt himself starting to like this girl. It might be nice to have somebody around who didn't take everything as seriously as Marty, or Theo either.

"Ah. Indeed." Evangeline leaned back in her chair, looking relieved. "That is what we have come to find, Mr. Hodge. The Quill. Where is it?"

"Don't you know?" Mr. Hodge looked surprised.

"We do not." Evangeline's face grew even more serious than usual, and her dark eyes focused sharply on Charley Hodge's face. "There has been . . . some trouble, Mr. Hodge. I do not want to go into details. But we must recover the Eagle's Quill as quickly as possible, and we need your help. Please tell us where it is."

Blinking, Charley Hodge spread his hands out, palms up. "I—I don't have any idea," he said.

Evangeline's shoulders dropped ever so slightly. Theo's face didn't change, but Marty sighed, and Sam groaned to himself. Of course it wouldn't be easy. Nothing to do with the Founders was ever easy.

Charley Hodge explained that, about two hundred years ago, his ancestor, Josiah Hodge, had been part of the Corps of Discovery, led by Lewis and Clark. It was the first formal attempt by the new American government to explore this part of the country. Josiah had not only been an explorer, however. He had a secret mission—to safeguard Thomas Jefferson's Quill.

Hodge's family had kept the Quill safely in their home for many years. "But around the Civil War something happened—I don't know what, and my dad didn't know either," Charley Hodge said. "But two Founders came, saying they were descendants of Jefferson. They took the Quill and hid it somewhere else, somewhere safe. My family wasn't told where. All we were told is to help anyone who came looking. Anyone with the right tattoos, that is. Like you."

"James Randolph would know where to look," Evangeline said, tapping her fingers on the arm of her chair in frustration. "But he is . . . unavailable."

"Climbing Mount Everest," Sam said.

"Perhaps not literally, Mr. Solomon. But, yes, in Nepal. So we shall . . ." Evangeline let her sentence trail off.

"What?" Abby asked, looking up from her seat by the fire. She had a thin, eager face with a scattering of freckles across milky skin, and she looked ready to jump up and start hunting for the Quill right then and there. "What's your plan?"

"We don't exactly . . ." Evangeline trailed off again.

"A *plan* makes this hunt sound a lot more organized than it's been so far," Sam said. "But now we know what we're looking for, right? That's something."

"Absolutely right." Evangeline sat up straighter. "And we have friends and allies that we did not have two hours ago."

"Of course you do." Anita Hodge spoke up for the first time. "Ms. Temple—"

"Please, call me Evangeline."

"Evangeline, then. We can tell something is wrong." Anita's voice and her eyes were warm and reassuring. "You don't need to tell us what—we won't ask. But we'll help you all we can." She stood up. "And right now, I think the best way to help is to get you dinner, and beds to sleep in, so we can all start to figure out this problem with fresh minds in the morning."

"Ms. Hodge—Anita." Evangeline smiled up at her. "You are perfectly correct."

"Then I will get some food cooking. Charley, you finish feeding the horses. And Abby, show our guests to their
rooms."

Sam and Theo got a room together, with thick patchwork
quilts on the bunk beds and posters of the wildlife in Glacier
National Park—wolves, grizzly bears, mountain lions. Marty
got her own room across the hall, and Abby showed Evangeline to a bigger guest room on the other side of the house,
with its own bathroom and shower. Evangeline wanted to
rest before dinner, so Abby turned to the three others.

"Come on! I'll show you around the ranch," she said.
Her eyes met Sam's, and she smiled. "There's some cool old
stuff. I bet you'd like to see it."

Theo trailed silently behind, Marty asked a million
questions about Thomas Jefferson, and Sam tried to pay
attention. "The house was designed to look something like
Thomas Jefferson's plantation, right, Abby?" Marty said,
following closely on Abby's heels.

"Sure, I guess," Abby said. "My dad knows more than
I do about the history of this place. But the hallway out
front is supposed to be the same—"

"As the front entrance in Monticello!" Marty interrupted. "I could tell. It's an octagon, and it's got the inlaid
wooden floor and the clock over the door."

"Sure!" Abby said, her voice bright and cheerful. "Just
the same!" Sam recognized that voice. It was the one he

used when he was trying to convince a teacher that *of
course* he'd done his homework.

"Jefferson designed that clock himself, you know,"
Marty went on. "And he—"

"I'll show you the musket Josiah Hodge carried on
the Lewis and Clark Expedition," Abby broke in. "Dad
keeps it in the dining room." She had figured out Marty
in no time at all, Sam thought, impressed. She knew the
only way to get a word in edgewise was to interrupt, since
Marty never stopped for a breath.

Abby led them through the kitchen, where the smell of
hamburgers sizzling in a skillet made Sam's mouth water, and
into the dining room. There was a big table of smooth, dark
wood in the center of the room, surrounded by eight chairs.

On one wall, over another fireplace, was an ancient-
looking gun. To Sam, it looked like something from
a play—could it really have fired bullets? It was hard to
imagine.

Beside the musket, in a heavy gold frame, was an old
map, its parchment protected by thick glass. "That shows
where the Lewis and Clark Expedition went," Abby told
them. "You can see how close they came to where we are."

"What's this thing?" Sam asked, as Marty darted off to
examine the map up close.

"Um . . ." Abby frowned at the contraption Sam had
noticed. It stood on a long, narrow sideboard below the

musket. "I forget its name. My dad will know. It's some kind of—"

"A polygraph!" Marty exclaimed, rushing back to their side. Theo came to look too.

"Huh? A Revolutionary War lie detector?" Sam asked. "What did they do, wire somebody up to this and tickle them with the quill if they told a lie?"

Abby giggled. Marty sighed. "Not a lie detector, Sam!" she said, like a disappointed teacher.

"I think he was joking, Marty," Abby told her. She kept her mouth straight, but she shot a quick glance at Sam, and her eyes were bright with amusement.

Marty's gaze went quickly from Abby to Sam and then back to the machine on the table. Above a flat wooden platform a quill pen was poised, held in an intricate system of wires and levers, as though it were about to start writing all by itself. An inkpot of thick, carved glass stood nearby— Sam guessed you were supposed to dip the quill in that. A tall, elegant silver candlestick had been placed on each side.

Theo moved away, as if he'd lost interest, and went across the room to stand with his hands in his pockets, staring out of a window that showed a view of stables and corrals and all the buildings of a working ranch.

"It's a copying machine," Marty explained. If she'd been at all bothered by the fact that Abby got Sam's joke while she didn't, the joy of history seemed to have washed it from her mind. "See, you put a sheet of paper—or parch-ment, I guess—on the platform. Then you write with one quill, and the other quill follows the movements precisely, creating a second copy."

"What other quill?" Sam asked.

"Well, there should be another quill. There. See how there's a holder?" Marty pointed. "But it's empty."

Anita's voice drifted in from the room next door. "Dinner in two minutes! Abby, go tell your father. The rest of you kids, why don't you come in here and help me get the table set?"

"Thomas Jefferson used a polygraph every day," Marty said as they gathered up plates and napkins in the kitchen and took them to the dining room. "To make copies of all his letters and documents. He thought it was a great scien-tific advancement."

"A Revolutionary War Xerox machine, huh? A lie detector would have been cooler," Sam said, folding napkins.

Along with the hamburgers, dinner was corn on the cob, coleslaw, baked beans, and heaping bowls of ice cream for dessert. Charley Hodge told them stories about the Lewis and Clark Expedition. Marty chimed in often to add details. Abby, sitting next to Sam, turned to whisper to him. "I've heard all of these before," she told him. "The next one is going to be about the moose that trampled a canoe."

Sure enough, the next thing Charley said was, "And one evening, just as everybody was settling in for the night, a moose came tearing out of the woods, straight for the river where the canoes were moored. And then—"

Sam had to cover his mouth with one arm to smother his laughter. Theo, meanwhile, ate three hamburgers in silence, chewing mechanically, as if he hardly noticed the food. Evangeline, listening attentively to Charley's stories, glanced at Theo from time to time, worry in her eyes. Then she would turn back to Charley and ask another question that would start a whole new story.

After dinner was over and the dishes were washed, Sam found to his surprise that he couldn't stop yawning. Anita Hodge noticed, and before Sam could figure out what had happened, she'd sent all four of the kids off to bed.

Sam lay on the top bunk, warm under his quilt. His stomach was stuffed, his thoughts slow and sleepy, his body starting to relax. Not even the gaze of the ferocious predators on the walls could bother him.

This wasn't going to be so bad, Sam thought. Not anywhere near as difficult and dangerous as finding Ben Franklin's key had been. In Death Valley, he and Marty and Theo had been all alone, thrown into the crazy puzzles and deadly traps of Ben Franklin's vault before they even knew what they were doing. This time was different. They had Evangeline and the Hodges to help them, a place to stay, and it looked like Gideon Arnold hadn't managed to follow them from Death Valley. Because if he had, surely they'd have seen some sign of him by now.

So, for the moment at least, they were safe. Sam sighed and closed his eyes.

The next day they'd have to start figuring out where the Eagle's Quill was hidden and what kind of traps might be guarding it. All that would be a puzzle—just what Sam was good at.

Puzzles were for the morning, though. Right now, all Sam had to do was rest. He listened to Theo turn over once, twice, and then a third time in the bunk below. And he felt himself slide peacefully into sleep.

At least, until the explosions began.

CHAPTER THREE

It sounded as if a bulldozer had slammed into a wall of the bedroom.

Sam threw himself off the bunk, half climbed and half slid down the ladder, stepped on Theo, and rolled to the floor. "What's going on?" he asked, staggering to his feet.

"We've got to get out," Theo said, not bothering to answer Sam's question. Sam stuffed his feet into his sneakers as Theo headed for the door. The room was almost pitch black—it must still be the middle of the night. Just before he reached it, it swung open. Marty was on the other side, visible in the dim light from the hallway. Her glasses were askew, her hair rumpled, and her eyes wide.

"We've got to get to Evangeline," Theo said, pushing past Marty into the hallway. "Follow me, you two." Sam got out of the room just as a door opposite theirs burst open to reveal Abby in a pair of sweatpants and a T-shirt, her fair hair tumbled loose around her shoulders.

"What's that noise?" she asked, voice trembling.

"We don't know," Sam told her.

"We've got to get somewhere safe!" Abby looked around wildly. The explosions seemed to have stopped, for the moment. Sam's ears rang with the silence.

"We will. Don't worry," Sam told her.

Then he heard footsteps. Running footsteps.

"Or maybe worry," Sam whispered, jerking his head up as two men came around the corner of the hallway.

They didn't look friendly. They had thick black jackets, backpacks that were heavy with gear, and grim expressions on their faces. "It's the kids! Grab them!" the one in back yelled. He seemed to fill up the hallway, and on his face Sam glimpsed a scar that ran from eyebrow to jaw.

Sam recognized him at once. He was one of Flintlock's men, the one named Jed, who had helped to corner Sam, Theo, and Marty in a cavern under Death Valley.

Theo stepped forward, pushing Marty behind him. "Come on!" Sam yelped. "Run!"

But instead of running, Theo turned sideways to the oncoming men and thrust one arm out. The guy in front couldn't stop in time. He pretty much ran into Theo's fist, and he fell to the ground with a groan, clutching at his nose.

But that left Jed, and he was pulling a gun out of a holster inside his jacket.

"Theo! Watch out!" Marty shouted.

To Sam's shock, it was Abby who stepped forward this time. One leg bent, the knee drawing up. Her leg snapped forward and her foot connected with Jed's wrist just as his gun was coming forward to point at Theo's head.

To Sam's astonishment, he heard bone crack. Jed yelled. Abby kicked again, this time hitting his knee, and he fell.

"*Now* run!" Abby said. "Follow me!"

The four of them turned and took off down the hallway, Abby in the lead.

Abby led them through the kitchen and into the dining room, where she skidded to a stop. Sam nearly ran into her, and Marty plowed into Sam.

Another man in black, a walkie-talkie in his hand, turned away from examining the map of the Lewis and Clark Expedition. He smiled. "In here," he said into his walkie-talkie before clipping it back onto his belt. "All right now," he told the kids. "No need to make a fuss. Just come with me."

Abby backed away from him, pushing Sam and Marty back too, so they bumped into Theo. "Let's go," the man said calmly, taking a step forward.

Sam was pretty sure he did not want to go anywhere with this guy. Without pausing to think, he grabbed one of the silver candlesticks that stood next to the polygraph and hurled it at the man's head. The guy ducked. With vague memories of backyard football games stirring in his head, Sam dove for his knees. They both went down, and the back of the man's head bounced off the wall with a heavy, solid thud. He hit the ground and lay still.

"Hey!" Sam beamed, scrambling up. "You see that? Somebody notify the Football Hall of Fame!"

"This way!" Abby said, ignoring Sam. She headed for a door across the room, one Sam had not noticed before. But before she reached it, two more men in black jackets burst in from the kitchen. One was Jed, holding his gun in his left hand and limping a bit. The other had a seriously bloody nose. Both looked as if they had payback on their minds.

Jed made a grab at Abby, who dodged. Theo seized the second candlestick. Marty, though, had a different idea. In two steps she was at the wall where Josiah Hodge's musket hung, and she grabbed it. "Hands up!" she shouted, swinging the musket around to point at the two intruders. "Or I'll shoot!"

It was ridiculous, but the two men were so startled that they stood still for a second, blinking with shock. And a second was all Theo needed to use his candlestick to crack the one with the bloody nose across the side of the head, knocking him to the floor.

Jed, recovering from the shock of finding himself on the business end of a two-hundred-year-old antique, swore and lunged at Theo. Marty yelped in alarm and threw the musket straight at him. It thumped into his shoulder, and he staggered, his bad knee giving way under him. He fell, and Theo leaped out of his way.

"Follow me! Now!" Abby shouted, charging for the door a second time.

Sam was on her heels, with Marty behind him and Theo bringing up the rear. Jed scrambled up and followed, just in time to whack into the door as Theo slammed it shut behind him. Theo braced his back against the door and dug his heels into the floor. Sam heard the thump and saw the door shake as Jed threw his weight against it.

"Does this—lock?" Theo gasped, and Abby darted back to his side and did something to the doorknob.

"There!" she said, and Theo stepped away. A heavy body clobbered the door again, and the hinges groaned, but the lock held.

They were in a hallway Sam did not recognize. He was pretty sure it hadn't been on Abby's tour yesterday. Abby took off running again, and they followed her as something hit the door for a third time. They heard wood crack.

Halfway down the hallway, Abby stopped. She slammed her palm flat against a patch of wall that, to Sam, looked no different from any other part of the hallway.

"Abby, what—?" Sam wheezed, coming up behind her. A section of the wall slid aside, revealing a dark rectangle of doorway. Sam was startled enough to jump back, stepping on Marty's toe.

"In!" Abby disappeared through the doorway. Sam followed, with Marty and Theo close behind. The door slid shut with a heavy, solid thud, and lights came up all around them just as gunshots exploded in the hallway outside.

"Look," Abby said, pointing to a screen over the doorway. It was a clunky-looking monitor, covered with dust, and on it a grainy black-and-white movie was playing. A huge man with a scarred face, a pistol in his left hand, kicked open a ruined doorway and stepped through it. He looked around blankly and started running down a hallway, favoring one knee. In moments he'd shoved his way through a doorway at the far end and disappeared.

"That was Jed," Marty said, amazement ringing in her voice. "He—he didn't see the door, I guess."

Abby shook her head. "It's very hard to see, unless you know where it is. And anyway, he couldn't get in. That door is reinforced seven ways from Sunday. Bulletproof too."

Sam turned to stare at her. What kind of a girl was Abby, who could break a bad guy's wrist with one kick? What kind of a place was Caractacus Ranch, with a secret hideout straight out of James Bond?

The room had more than a bulletproof door, he realized as he looked around. There were multiple screens on the walls, each showing a different view of the house. There were shelves with bottles of water, canned goods, and boxes of protein bars and chocolate bars. There were cots and blankets, winter coats and boots, sweatpants and hoodies folded neatly on a shelf. There was even a shelf with board games—Boggle, Scrabble, checkers, chess, Monopoly.

You could survive a siege in this place.

"Abby?" Sam asked. "What *is* all this?"

But Abby was not listening. She was looking up at the screens, and she made a sharp little whimpering sound.

Sam looked up quickly too, and Theo let out his breath between his teeth.

One of the screens on the walls showed a view from outside the front entrance to the ranch. One next to it had a view of the door that led from the kitchen out the back. Sam saw that both doors just—didn't exist anymore. There were merely holes in the walls where they had been. That had been what awakened them, Sam realized—the doors being blown to bits.

But that wasn't what had captured everyone's attention. Another screen showed the octagonal hallway near the front door, and there, standing near a pile of rubble that had once been a wall of the house, were Abby's parents and Evangeline.

"My mom and dad," Abby whispered, her voice quavering.

"It'll be okay," Sam said to her. Which was about the stupidest thing he could have said. Everything was clearly very far from okay, and all four of them knew perfectly well that things might not be okay ever again.

Charley Hodge had his arm around his wife. Evangeline stood stiffly by herself, her face cold and angry. Men in black jackets surrounded them. Another man stood a little distance away. He seemed to be talking on a cell phone, and Sam recognized him. He had dark hair, a rugged face lined from sun and wind, and thick eyebrows drawn down in a scowl that seemed permanent.

"Flintlock!" Sam whispered. Marty gasped. Theo just stared, his eyes narrow, his whole body as rigid as if he'd been carved out of stone.

They'd met Flintlock in Death Valley. He wasn't just hired muscle, like Jed and the others who'd chased them through the ranch. Flintlock had brains, and even worse, he had a close relationship with his boss. If he was here, Gideon Arnold could not be far behind.

Flintlock nodded and put his phone away. Sam could see his mouth moving, but there was no sound. It was easy to guess what he'd said, though, from what happened next.

Flintlock's men took hold of Abby's parents and Evangeline, and tied their hands behind their backs. The three adults were forced to sit down against a wall that was more or less in one piece, and two men with guns stayed to guard them.

"Leave them alone," Abby whispered angrily, her hands clenched into fists by her side. "Don't you dare. Don't you dare . . ."

But they did dare. The rest of Flintlock's men fanned out all over the house.

The screens showed what was happening. The men kicked open cupboards, hauled down bookcases, and knocked furniture over. In the bedrooms they yanked everything out of the closets. In the kitchen, they dumped shelves of food on the floor. Wherever they went, they kicked at the walls and seemed to be listening to the sound. They were looking for the safe room, Sam realized. His throat felt tight, and it was hard to swallow. *They're hunting us down . . .*

"They won't find us," Abby said, her eyes still on the screen. "Yeah, good luck, you slimy pieces of trash. You aren't going to get in here."

"I really, really hope you're right," Sam told her.

The search seemed to go on for hours, but a digital clock on the walls showed that it had only been about forty-five minutes when Flintlock's men returned to the octagonal hallway, shaking their heads.

Flintlock frowned. He took out his cell phone again, made a quick call, and nodded.

Then, with one hand, Flintlock picked up a small table that was lying on its side, set it upright, and pulled a piece of paper out of a pocket. He wrote on the paper and then looked up. He smiled.

Flintlock must have spotted the security camera that was giving them their image. He walked toward it, his face looming larger and larger. Sam fought the urge to step backward. He knew Flintlock couldn't get to them in here, but still . . .

Flintlock held up the piece of paper. They could clearly read the words he had scrawled on it.

Don't call the police, or things will get messy.

Flintlock held the paper up long enough to be sure they had gotten a good look at his message. Then he crumpled it and dropped it to the floor. He took something black and rectangular out of his pocket and held that up for them to see. Then he laid it on the table where he had written his message.

Flintlock walked toward the hole in the wall, jerking his head at his men.

The armed men pulled Evangeline and the Hodges to their feet and shoved them outside. Abby gasped. Sam swung his gaze to a different screen, one that showed Flintlock getting into a van parked in the driveway. He and the others watched as Evangeline and the Hodges were forced into the back of a second van. Doors were slammed shut.

Slowly and sedately, with no spinning wheels or scattered gravel, the vans drove away.

Back in the safe room, Sam was slowly shaking his head, trying to get his brain around everything that had just happened. He'd been sleeping peacefully in a comfortable bed, thinking that everything was going to be—well, not easy, maybe, but more or less okay. And then explosions, panic, and finally disaster. What were they going to do now?

He looked around at the others. Marty had her arms hugged tightly around herself. Theo's face was expression-less; he might have been furious or terrified or thinking about his ten favorite Netflix movies. Sam just couldn't tell. Abby flopped down against a wall, her head drooping down, hiding her face. Sam thought he saw her shoulders shaking.

"Hey." Awkwardly, Sam knelt down next to her. "Hey, Abby, look. Try not to worry. I know you're scared, but—"

"Scared?" Abby's head came up, her blond hair whip-ping back. "Scared? Forget scared. I am going to *kill* those guys. I swear I'll kill them. They wrecked my house. They took my parents. I'm going to make them pay."

"Whoa." Sam sat back a little. Apparently Abby didn't really need comforting. "Okay. Right. Making them pay, I'm on board, sure." He decided not to mention that Abby's super-powered karate kicks might not be enough.

"Should we . . . go out?" Marty said, a little shakily.

Theo shook his head, his eyes still on the screens. "Wait. It could be a trap."

Sam sighed. He reached up to one of the shelves and pulled down a box of Milky Ways. If they had to sit around and wait . . .

"Sam, really. Now?" Marty scowled at him.

Sam ripped off a wrapper. "You have a better idea? Want to play Monopoly? I'll let you be the shoe."

Marty sat down against a different wall, as far from Abby and Sam as she could get.

"So, Abby," Sam said around a mouthful of chocolate and caramel. "You've always had this room here? In case there's a nuclear war or a zombie apocalypse or something?"

Abby was glaring up at the screens, along with Theo, but at Sam's questions she looked over at him and nodded.

"I didn't know about the safe room until last year," she said. "My dad told me then. He told me about the Quill too. He takes it seriously, Sam. He said we had to be prepared for anything."

Sam looked around at the shelves stocked with survival gear. They were prepared for anything, all right. "And did he teach you all those black belt moves?" he asked.

She shrugged. "Brown belt, actually. I've been going to martial arts classes since I was a kid. My dad always insisted. I never really knew why. Now I do." She sighed, staring up at the wreckage of her home on the screen. "Give me one of those candy bars, Sam."

Sam obliged.

"And tell me who that guy is. The one who has my mom and dad."

"His name is Flintlock," Sam said, swallowing the last of his candy. "He works for a man named Gideon Arnold."

They watched the screens while Sam told Abby a short version of what had happened to them in Death Valley, and how they'd escaped from Benjamin Franklin's vault, narrowly avoiding capture by Flintlock and Arnold.

In the black-and-white images on the monitors, a light wind blew dead leaves and scraps of paper through the open space of the octagonal hallway. Apart from that, nothing moved.

"Theo?" Sam said at last. "We can't stay in here forever." He looked around at the stocked shelves. "Or, well, we could, but . . ." But they couldn't. Not when Flintlock and Gideon Arnold had Evangeline and Abby's parents in their clutches.

"It could still be a trap," Theo said.

"Yeah, it could." Sam nodded. "But if we haven't spotted the trap by now, I don't think we're going to. See, either there's no trap, or there's one we can't figure out. So we go out and it's fine, or we go out and we deal with the trap once we find out if there is one. Because we can't deal with it in here."

Theo looked at Sam as if he were a little bit surprised. "Sam Solomon logic," he said, shaking his head.

"It's unique, but it does do the trick sometimes," Marty said, getting to her feet. "He's right, in that bizarre Sam way. Come on."

Abby nodded, getting up as well. She flipped a switch on the wall near the door, and it slid smoothly open.

They picked their way through the disaster that had been Caractacus Ranch only a few hours ago. Nobody jumped out to grab them. No bombs exploded, no trap doors opened beneath their feet. Sam felt jumpy enough to be ready for anything, but when nothing happened he felt . . . even jumpier.

They gathered in the ruins of the octagonal hallway, and the four of them stared at the object Flintlock had left on the small table for them to see.

"Is it a walkie-talkie?" Sam asked, picking it up.

"Sam!" Marty yelped. "That could have been booby-trapped. Don't be an idiot!"

"It's a satellite phone," Theo said.

The phone rang.

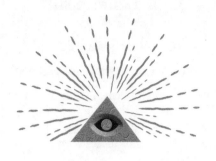

CHAPTER FOUR

Sam jumped and nearly dropped the phone. He couldn't help it. The sudden noise, together with Marty's comment about booby traps, had rattled him. It rang again. "What do I do?" he asked, as panicked as if he'd never seen a phone before.

"Answer it, you moron!" Marty told him.

Sam blinked at the phone's screen and poked at a flashing green button. The ringing stopped. He cautiously lifted the phone to his ear.

"Um, hello?"

"Mr. Solomon, I presume."

Sam felt something cold and heavy, like a hard-packed ball of slush, thud into the pit of his stomach. He'd know that smooth, precise voice anywhere. Gideon Arnold.

"Hold on. Let me put you on speaker," Sam said. He couldn't believe what an idiot he sounded like. He pushed another button. Arnold's voice rang out into the ruined hallway.

"Find the Quill," Arnold said, and somehow the fact that his words were so few made them even more menacing. "If there are puzzles, solve them. If there are traps, disarm them. I have no interest in difficulties or excuses. Once you have the Quill in your possession, use this phone to call me. If you do all of this, you may see your friend and relatives alive once more."

And the phone went dead.

"What? Wait!" Sam stared at the phone and shook it, as if that would bring Arnold back.

"Give it to me." Theo held out a hand. He tapped at the phone's buttons. "There's one number in the contacts section. It must be Arnold's."

"Great. So we can call the psychopath anytime we want," Sam said, shaking his head.

"We've got to do it." Abby was staring at the phone as if it might jump out of Theo's hand and bite her. "We've got to find that Quill! He's going to kill my parents!"

"It'll be okay, Abby," Marty said, turning to her. "Just calm down. I know this is all really crazy, but—"

"I do not *want* to calm down," Abby answered, narrowing her eyes at Marty. "That guy has my parents. He's the

one you met in Death Valley, right? The one whose ancestor was Benedict Arnold?"

"Yeah, that's the one," Sam agreed.

"So he's really insane." Abby turned to Sam. "He'd
really kill my parents. And your friend, Evangeline—he'd
kill her too?"

Sam hesitated.

"Gideon Arnold will kill anyone who gets in his way,"
Theo said. "Never doubt that."

"Then we've got to do what he said." Abby looked
fierce. "Come on! Let's go!"

"Let's go where?" Sam asked, bewildered.

"Look for clues," Abby answered. "This house has been
here since Josiah Hodge brought the Quill out west. Somewhere there's a clue. And we need to find it."

So they looked for clues. It wouldn't have been
easy if the house had been in decent shape, since they
didn't have a single idea of what they were looking
for. But as it was, they were looking for *something* in a
house that looked as if an earthquake had hit it. It was
hopeless.

They picked up fallen furniture, collected scattered
papers, and looked inside broken knickknacks. While they
did all this, Marty talked. Sam had known Marty less than a
week. But it was long enough to realize that Marty reacted
to stress with words. Lots of words.

"Thomas Jefferson died on the Fourth of July. Did you know that?" she asked. Sam was picking up books from the living room floor while Abby crawled into empty cupboards, tapping the walls to look for a secret hiding place.

"Nope." Sam dropped a thick book on fly-fishing onto a pile he was creating of "Things That Are Not Going to Help at All."

"So did John Adams. The exact same day. Isn't that bizarre?"

"Uh-huh." Sam picked up another book, a Civil War history. Theo heaved a bookcase upright so Sam would have somewhere to put the books that were not going to help.

"So Caractacus Ranch is designed to look like Monticello, right, Abby?" Marty went on. Abby grunted a yes as she crawled out of a cupboard. "Josiah Hodge had seen Monticello, probably. He would have known what it looked like. It's an amazing place. I went there on a school trip last year. Beautiful. Jefferson was really into geometry. Shapes and angles. Well, you can't design a house without caring about geometry, obviously . . ."

Thomas Jefferson was starting to sound like a real geek to Sam. But even as he shared a sideways glance and an eye roll with Abby, he had to admit that geometry wasn't so bad. It could help solve a puzzle, that was for sure, if you knew how many degrees were in a right angle or how to calculate the radius of a circle.

Marty had flopped down on a window seat whose cushion had been shredded. Polyester stuffing drifted up into her lap. "Octagons especially. He based a lot of Monticello on an octagon pattern. That central hall, for a start. Just like the one you have here, Abby. Eight sides. It created a pattern that he really liked . . ."

Sam dropped another book onto his pile and tuned Marty's voice out. An idea was tickling at the back of his brain.

Pawing through all the stuff in the house was no good. It was like staring at that giant map in the tourist center, trying to come up with a clue. That wasn't a puzzle; it was just a pile of information. A puzzle was not like that. A puzzle had hints or clues. Something to catch your eye, something to give you a starting place.

Often that starting place was something that didn't quite fit. That stood out. That caught your attention or that seemed just a little bit wrong.

Something a little bit wrong. Sam lifted a hand. "Marty, say that again."

"Say what? About Thomas Jefferson's recipe for ice cream?"

"No, not that. About geometry. About shapes. About—"

"Octagons? Like the front hall?"

The front hall. Sam had been stuck in that safe room for two hours, staring up at the monitors. One screen had showed the hallway where Evangeline and Abby's parents had been held.

Jefferson really liked octagons. Octagons had eight sides. And something wasn't quite right here. Something Sam had seen on that monitor . . .

"It's wrong!" he blurted and ran out of the room.

The others followed him as he skidded to a stop in the hallway, turning slowly around in a circle. "Sam? What is it? It's a sugar rush from all that candy, isn't it?" Marty asked. "Or maybe it really is PTSD."

"No! It's an octagon! The hallway! I mean, it's not!" Sam grinned widely. They'd gotten it! He and Marty together had figured it out. The first step of the puzzle, the place to start!

"Look, either it's an octagon or it isn't," Marty said. "It can't be both."

"It's supposed to be an octagon, but look! Count the walls! This room only has seven sides! It's a seven-sides-a-gon."

"A heptagon." Marty's eyes brightened, and she turned in a slow circle, looking at the ruined hallway. "Seven sides. Seven Founders. Sam, that's it! Ben Franklin, Thomas Jefferson, John Adams . . ."

"Alexander Hamilton, James Madison, John Jay . . . ," Theo chimed in, nodding.

"John Jay? Didn't he play for the Red Sox?"

"Sam! Be serious!" Marty glared. But suddenly, briefly, Abby smiled. She got it, Sam realized. Marty talked when she was nervous. Sam joked when he was on the verge of solving a puzzle. He could feel it at this moment, that electric fizz of excitement when all the pieces were about to slide into place.

"And the last one, of course, is our old friend, George Washington!" Sam bowed toward Theo.

"So we're looking for . . . Thomas Jefferson's wall? Maybe?" Marty frowned, shaking her head. "I don't see anything specific . . ."

"Let's hope Tom's wall wasn't the one that got blown to pieces," Sam said. Theo had moved over to the walls of the room and was walking slowly along them, running his fingers lightly over the white-painted paneling.

"Abby? Any ideas? You've lived here all your life," Sam said.

Abby shook her head. "My dad never told me anything special about this room. Maybe he thought I wasn't ready or something."

"Or maybe he just didn't know," Sam added.

"Or maybe there's nothing after all." Marty chewed her lip, looking worried.

"There's something." Theo stopped at the wall that was farthest from the room's outside door—or where that door had once been. "Look. Well, don't look. It's hard to see. But come and feel it. Right here."

Sam came to Theo's side and rubbed his fingers gently over the wall where Theo showed him. He could feel shallow grooves, lines that had been carved, very lightly, into the wall's paneling, and then painted over. They were so faint they were hard to see, but Sam traced them carefully with his fingertips. A triangle. No, a pyramid. A pyramid with something inside it—a feather with a curled top. A quill.

"This is it!" Sam grinned with triumph and slapped his palm on the Founders' symbol, as if he were giving the wall a high five. "Thomas Jefferson's wall—whoa!"

The panel was shifting. He snatched his hand away as the panel slid aside, revealing a dark opening in the wall.

"What's in there?" Abby asked, coming to stare over Sam's shoulder.

"Theo, be careful," Marty warned, as Theo reached gingerly into the dark hole.

"There's something—I got it. Here!" Theo pulled his hand out, clutching two objects. He put those down on the little table where they'd found the satellite phone.

Sam studied the two objects, feeling his grin spread wider over his face. Things were pretty dire—Gideon Arnold had tracked them down, Evangeline and Abby's mom and dad were in danger—but he and Marty could still beat the Founders' puzzles. So that was something.

For a moment Sam thought the first thing Theo had recovered was a tiny clock, small enough to fit in the palm of his hand. Then he realized his mistake. The brass circle had letters around its edges, rather than numbers: N, S, E, W. North, south, east, west. It reminded him a bit of the sundial he and Theo and Marty had found on the top of a mountain in Death Valley, except for the slender needle that quivered and swung in its center. A compass!

The other thing—Sam had no idea. "What's that?" he asked as Marty picked the object up with gentle, cautious fingers.

"It's a wheel cipher," she told him.

"A cipher?" Sam was intrigued. He leaned closer to get a better look. A cipher was a code—and a code was a puzzle. It was the kind of thing Sam was good at.

It looked to Sam like a long cylinder made out of wood, with letters carved all around its edge. But when Marty handled it, Sam saw that it was actually a series of wooden disks, all threaded onto a metal rod so each could rotate independently of the others. Marty spun one disk gently with her finger.

"Thomas Jefferson invented this," she said in an awed tone. "He used it to send secret messages."

"How?" Sam's fingers itched to take it from her to see if he could figure it out. But he restrained himself.

"All the disks have the letters of the alphabet around the edge. So you spin the disks to spell out a message. One letter to each disk." Marty twisted the disks and arranged the letters.

"Then, to send your message, you write down the letters on a different line—maybe the one above." Marty pointed to a nonsense row of letters: HWD QH W PNNLXH. "You send your secret message to somebody, and they line up those letters on *their* cipher wheel and then look around the disk to see which line actually makes sense. So you can read—"

"SAM IS A DOOFUS," Sam read. Theo's mouth twitched very, very slightly. "Thanks, Marty. Thanks a lot."

"It makes sense that Josiah Hodge might have had one of those ciphers," Abby said. "After all, he was working for Thomas Jefferson."

"But what are we supposed to do with it?" Sam asked. "Send somebody a secret message, or decode one?"

"Somebody else would have to have a cipher wheel just like this one," Marty said. "Either to send us a message or to understand one that we sent."

Sam nodded. "I don't suppose you guys know of anybody in the world with a wheel cipher just like that one?" Nobody did. Sam shrugged and turned his attention back to the compass, watching the sensitive needle inside the case shiver and swing as he moved it. He turned it over and saw words inscribed on the wooden case. "'In matters of style, swim with the current,'" he read. "'In matters of principle, stand like a rock.'"

Abby's shoulders slumped. "What's that supposed to mean?"

"You know," Marty said. "If something isn't super important, like what kind of coat to wear, do what other people do. But—"

"But when something is important, don't change. Stick with your principles," Theo said, cutting Marty off. "Do what you believe is right."

"I know *that*." Abby looked impatient. "I *mean*, what is it telling us to do? How is it supposed to help find my parents?"

"I don't know, but—" Marty started to answer her.

"Which way is north?" Sam broke in, staring down at the compass in his hand.

"Sam, you're holding a compass, and you're asking which way is north?" Marty sighed.

"I'm serious." Sam kept his eyes on the compass. "Which way?"

"Well, the sun is rising *there*." Marty pointed out the door. "So that's east. So *that's* north." She pointed a different direction.

"Are you sure?"

"It's not like the sun is going to rise in the southwest today. Sam, what's up?"

"The compass doesn't point north." Sam looked up, feeling that fizzing excitement again.

"It has to," Marty insisted. "The earth's magnetic field—"

"Marty, it doesn't. It's pointing northeast."

"That's crazy."

"No, it's not." Sam grinned. "It's a clue."

Marty insisted on running back to her room for her own compass and using it to check against the antique one they'd found in the wall. Her sleek black compass pointed directly north, but the needle of the old one definitely swung in a different direction.

"Old TJ gave us a clue at last," Sam said. "The Quill has got to be northeast of here."

"Then let's go!" Abby looked ready to set off immediately.

"Hold it," Theo said. "Wait a minute."

"Wait?" Abby swung around to face him. "That Quill might be the only chance I have of seeing my parents again. What am I supposed to wait for? Why can't we start right away?"

"For one thing," Sam pointed out, "we're still wearing our pajamas."

CHAPTER FIVE

The four of them hurried back to their rooms to pull on warm clothes and hiking boots and stuff backpacks with essential supplies. Then they met outside what remained of the ranch's back door. The park was too big to explore on foot, Abby pointed out, and they might have to cover a lot of ground. They would need transportation.

Sam was really hoping that she meant a jeep, or perhaps a few ATVs, although his last experience on one of those, being chased across a desert by Gideon Arnold's hired thugs, hadn't been all that fun. Still it would be better than—

"Horses," Abby said. Sam groaned quietly, following her as she led them downhill toward the stables.

Once inside the stables, Abby quickly selected four mounts, leading them out of their stalls and hauling out saddles and bridles. Marty expertly saddled up a dark-brown mare with a black mane and tail. Abby said her name was Polly Peachum. "I used to take lessons once a week at this stable near our house. I loved it!" Marty said happily, stroking Polly on the nose.

Theo also seemed to know what to do with the saddle Abby handed him, putting it on a big gray horse and cinching it up tight. "That's Silveret," Abby told him. "You've ridden before?"

Theo nodded. "Wilderness camping. With my mom. In the summers." He took the bridle from Abby and turned his back on her to pull the complicated contraption over Silveret's face.

Abby saddled up another brown horse called Ethelinda for herself, which left a black beast who seemed to have a mean glint in her eye for Sam.

"Here you go." Abby handed Sam a bridle. Sam stared at it in dismay.

"What do I do with this?"

"You put it on the horse," Abby told him.

Sam eyed the horse, and turned to Abby with a look of wide-eyed dismay. "Which end?"

Abby's mouth twitched. "That's a joke, right?"

"Kind of."

"On second thought, I'll take that." She retrieved the bridle. "You haven't ridden much, have you?"

Sam considered telling her about Adam's birthday party, but it didn't seem like the moment. "No."

"Ever?"

"Ah, no."

"Okay. No sweat," Abby assured him. "Peggy's used to tenderfoots."

"Shouldn't that be tenderfeet? And 'Peggy'?"

"Peggy Waffington." Abby slapped the horse on the neck in a friendly way. Sam wondered if he could do that too, or if he'd get his arm bitten off. He also wondered who'd come up with these horses' names. Did it have to do with Thomas Jefferson, by any chance? Had *he* owned horses named Polly Peachum and Peggy Waffington? If Sam had known that back in the 1700s, he definitely would not have voted for the guy.

Theo and Marty had already taken their horses outside, and once Abby finished saddling up Peggy, she handed the reins to Sam and told him to lead the mare out into the yard. Sam tugged gingerly at the thin leather straps. Peggy rolled an eye and looked bored.

"Harder. She has to know you mean it," Abby told him as she led Ethelinda out.

"Right." Sam gave Peggy a stern look and pulled harder on the reins. Peggy huffed out a sigh and wandered slowly after him, clearly trying to make it seem that it was her own idea to walk outside, and it had nothing to do with the puny little human tugging on some pieces of leather connected to her head.

"Lead her to the mounting block," Abby called. "Over there."

Sam took Peggy over to the big square box, and, following Abby's instructions, climbed up on it. Theo and Marty and Abby were already on their horses, hopping up easily from the ground as if there were nothing to it. Sam looked at Peggy's broad black back doubtfully. She seemed a lot wider from up here than she had on the ground.

"Put your foot in the stirrups—no, your right foot!" Abby shouted to him. "And just swing your other leg over the saddle. Easy."

Sam did as she said. For one quick second he was on top of Peggy. The next second he was coming down on the ground with a thump.

"Hey! Did she buck me off?" Sam stared up at Peggy's bulk looming above him and scuttled back so she wouldn't step on his toes.

Marty was giggling wildly, and even Abby looked as if she were trying to stifle a smile. Theo had turned his head away.

"No. Not exactly," Abby said. "You just kind of . . . slid off. It's okay. Just get up—Peggy! Don't do that!"

"Hey! Get away from me!" Sam yelled. Peggy had suddenly become interested in the small human near her front hooves, which looked as wide across as dinner plates to Sam. She put her head down. A warm, velvety nose snuffled over Sam's face and investigated his shirt. Her mouth opened, and a wet pink tongue came out. There were teeth too, big yellow ones. Sam didn't know all that much about horses, but he was sure they weren't carnivorous. Pretty sure. Almost completely sure.

"I think she's going to eat me!" he yelped.

"Peggy! Knock it off!" Abby was swinging off her horse. "Sam, it's fine. She just—"

Peggy's lips lifted back over her teeth. Frozen, Sam stared in fascinated horror. He hadn't survived sneaking into Ben Franklin's vault and getting kidnapped by Gideon Arnold just to become the first human being eaten by a horse, had he?

Snap! Peggy's teeth closed on something in Sam's shirt pocket. She pulled it out. It was—licorice?

"She likes candy," Abby said, appearing underneath Peggy's chin, gripping the reins, and pulling the horse a few steps away. "Sorry, Sam. I should have warned you."

Sam got up shakily. "So we've got something in common, huh?" he asked, watching in disbelief as Peggy Waffington chomped up his licorice in a few bites. He reached into his pocket, found a leftover piece, and held it out gingerly.

"Keep your palm flat and let her take it off," Abby told him. "That way she won't bite your fingers. But don't be greedy, Peggy. That's it. You know candy's not good for you. Apples from now on!"

Sam did as Abby told him. Peggy nibbled the treat from his hand and snorted happily. Then she vigorously sniffed the rest of his pockets in case he was holding out on her.

"That's it, I swear, girl," Sam said. Obeying Abby's instructions, he tried mounting a second time, and this time he managed to stay on Peggy's back.

"Just tap her with your heels," Abby called to him as she led the way out of the corral, with Theo and Marty following her. "She's a trail ride horse—she'll follow the others. It's what she's used to doing."

"Listen," Sam told the horse as they walked out of the yard behind Theo, Marty, and Abby. "Let's make a deal. You don't toss me off, and I share my candy with you. Interested?"

Peggy flapped a black ear back at him in a way that made it clear he'd caught her attention, but he'd better make any deal worth her while.

"And I'm not calling you Peggy Waffington," Sam told her. "Because, come on. How about Snickers? That's my favorite candy bar. So: a much cooler name and half my stash. You're not going to get a better offer today."

Snickers sneezed, which Sam decided meant yes.

In a line, the horses headed along a well-worn path that crossed a green hillside and entered a dense forest, where it branched into three distinct trails heading off among the trees.

"Sam? You've got the compass?" Abby called from up ahead.

Sam did. He pulled the compass out of a pocket in his cargo pants and checked it. "The middle trail!" he yelled back. "That's northeast!"

The horses took them under the cover of thick trees. Pines and firs with heavy green needles towered overhead, and pinecones crunched under the horses' hooves. Sam found himself rocking a little with Snickers's movements, listening to the leather of the saddle creak beneath him. He kept the compass in his hand to be sure they were headed in the right direction, toward the Quill.

He kept an ear out for helicopters too, or airplanes, or jeeps, or ATVs that might suddenly be chasing them down. Gideon Arnold knew where they were. And how, exactly? Had he followed them from Death Valley? Had he figured out Ben Franklin's clue on his own? There was no way to know, and it didn't matter that much anyway, Sam realized. The important fact was that Arnold was here, and that meant danger was here too.

But nobody attacked them, unless you counted the mosquitoes that buzzed in Sam's ears and tried to crawl

under his collar. Slowly the skin on Sam's back stopped
crawling, and he stopped twitching at every rustle in the
bushes or every squawk from a bird overhead.

Apparently no bad guys were stalking them. Thinking
it over, Sam supposed that made sense. They were doing
exactly what they'd been told to do. Like good little boys
and girls, they were heading off to find the Quill. Gideon
Arnold would not want to interfere with that.

Sam should have been relieved to know that Flintlock
wasn't going to jump out of the bushes at them, and Jed
wasn't going to swing down from a tree like Tarzan. But it
left a bad taste in his mouth, the idea that they were tamely
following Gideon Arnold's orders.

And once the kids found the Quill—if they found the
Quill—what then? Would they use that satellite phone and
call Arnold up like they were old buddies or something?
*Hey, Gideon, come and pick up your Quill. And could we have
Evangeline and Abby's mom and dad back, please? Thanks!*

That didn't seem like such a good idea. The whole
point of getting their hands on the Founders' artifacts in
the first place was to keep them out of Gideon Arnold's
clutches. But what else could they do?

First things first, Sam decided. Find the Quill. Then
figure out what to do with it.

Ahead of him, Ethelinda, Silveret, and Polly made their
way through a small creek that crossed the path, their

hooves splashing in the water. Snickers got to the creek and stopped dead. Sam lurched forward and nearly impaled his stomach on the saddle horn.

"Sam! Keep up!" Marty called from ahead.

"Tap her with your heels!" Abby yelled. Sam did so. Snickers snorted. It sounded like a laugh.

The other three horses disappeared around a bend in the path. Sam groaned. Cautiously, he tugged one foot out of the stirrup and wiggled around until he was lying across Snickers's back. He flopped to the ground, which seemed like a long way down, and staggered a bit when he landed. Luckily nobody was watching this except Snickers. And that was embarrassing enough.

Grimly, Sam waded across the creek. The water only came up to his ankles. "I can't believe you're making me do this," he told Snickers. "It's barely five inches deep. You're a wimp, you know that?"

He dug a hand into his backpack and pulled out a roll of mint Life Savers. He popped one in his mouth and held another out on his open palm.

"Snickers? Come on, girl. You know you want it."

Snickers splashed eagerly across the stream to Sam's side, nosing the candy out of his hand and crunching it up happily.

"Not a word to anybody about this," Sam muttered. He got a foot in the stirrup again, hopped two or three times, and, clinging to the saddle horn, sort of crawled up the horse's side. Once he was up, Snickers seemed to notice that she had been left behind. She trotted after the other horses, bouncing Sam wildly up and down.

"I never—signed—up—for—this!" he gasped. Deadly traps, killer puzzles, bad guys with guns, sure thing. But the Founders had not warned him there would be sugar-crazed horses to deal with!

The horses walked steadily for hours, taking them deeper into the forest and farther away from Caractacus Ranch and anything that might resemble civilization. It felt strangely peaceful, except for the fact that Sam's butt was starting to ache. The muscles in his legs were announcing that they were unhappy with their working conditions and about to go on strike. If Snickers was doing all the work, how come Sam was getting all the pain?

When the sun was directly overhead, they came out from under the cover of the trees and paused at the top of a steep, narrow trail that zigzagged its way down a rocky hillside. At the bottom of the slope, a swift river churned and tumbled between giant rocks. "We'd better walk the horses," Abby said. Sam slithered off Snickers's back gratefully, only to find that his legs were oddly rubbery when he hit the ground.

Each of them took hold of the reins and began making their way downhill, Marty in front, Theo and Abby behind her, and Sam bringing up the rear. Just as Snickers snorted in his ear, Sam heard Theo ask Abby a question.

"Have any other Founders ever come to the ranch?"

"No," Abby said, picking her way over a scree of loose rock and coaxing Ethelinda after her. "You're the first. My dad . . ." She hesitated a moment and then went on, steadying her voice. "My dad used to talk about how maybe we'd be the first Hodges since Josiah to meet a Founder."

Snickers nosed at Sam's backpack so hard that he nearly went sprawling. "Hey! Snickers! Cut that out!" He turned to face her sternly. The horse perked up when he met her gaze, and Sam sighed. He could guess what she wanted.

"Okay, okay." He dug the Life Savers out of the pack and offered her another one. "Just one at a time, hear me?"

It took the whole pack of Life Savers to get Snickers down the slope. All that time, in between muttered conversations with his horse, Sam could hear Abby talking to Theo. He heard "hard to believe" and "a real-life descendant of George Washington, honestly?" and "so you know about some artifact of his, where it's hidden and stuff?" Sam also heard grunts, those coming from Theo. The big guy had been talking even less than usual since they'd gotten to Montana, and that was saying something, Sam thought. He was surprised that Theo had struck up a conversation with Abby at all.

Just then Snickers nudged Sam's shoulder impatiently with her nose, and he handed her the second-to-last Life

Saver. Ahead of them, Marty had stopped on the last bit of flat ground before the river.

"The path ends here," she called back. "What next?"

It was a serious river too, deeper and faster than it had looked from the top of the slope. The water leaped over and churned around boulders that had probably fallen or rolled from the slopes of the mountains all around, and the sound of it rushing by was so loud they all had to raise their voices to be heard.

"Swim with the current!" Sam said.

"Swimming? In that?" Marty looked alarmed.

"That's what the compass said, remember?" Sam reminded her. "'In matters of style, swim with the current.' And the needle is pointing that way. Downstream." He held out the compass to show her.

"So that's the way we go." Marty dug a big map out of her overstuffed backpack and spread it out on a large, flat rock. "Look, this river heads pretty steadily northeast from here, so it should take us in the right direction. Too bad there's no path, but we can walk along the edge."

"The horses can't, though," Abby pointed out. "It's too rocky for them. One of them could throw a shoe or even break a leg."

"So what do we do with them?" Snickers stuck her nose in the back of Sam's collar and whooshed a warm breath down his neck. He jumped away from her.

"We send them home." Abby helped them turn the horses around on the narrow path so they were headed back up the trail they'd just come down. She tied up the reins so they would not hang loose and get tangled in the horses' feet, and then slapped each one on the rump. Startled, the horses snorted and flicked their tails, trotting back up the slope toward the forest.

"They'll head back for the stable," Abby said, watching them go. "That's where they get fed, so they like it. They know the way."

She looked a little sad, though, and Sam was surprised to find that he also felt a bit sorry to see the horses go. He was happy to be back on his own feet, no question, but the horses were their last connection to Caractacus Ranch and the outside world. Now it was just the four of them, all alone in a million acres of wilderness that held—somewhere—Thomas Jefferson's Quill.

They stopped for protein bars and water, sitting on rocks and watching the river flow by, and then got on their way.

The noise of the water made it too hard to talk, so they walked in silence. Mountains rose up on all sides, gray peaks, some splashed with snow, seeming high enough to snag the clouds. It was beautiful . . . if you weren't worried about scary Founder traps or crazy guys with guns.

Following Theo, Sam clambered over rocks and clomped along gravel flats that looked smooth but were hard going as the tiny stones shifted and gave way beneath his feet. This was taking too long, he thought, as he checked the compass for the millionth time. When he glanced behind him, he could see Abby and Marty struggling as well. They were making progress, but it was slow. Should they have kept the horses? Should they have found another way? Should they look for a trail where the walking would be easier?

Ahead of Sam, Theo raised an arm, signaling the rest to stop. He glanced back, mouthed "Stay here!" and moved ahead.

The river poured around a curve in its bed, and Theo disappeared around that curve. Abby and Marty, panting, caught up with Sam. "What's he doing?" Abby asked in Sam's ear.

Sam shrugged, hands out, palms up. In less than a minute, Theo was back. He waved at them to come on.

"What's up?" Sam called as soon as he was close enough for Theo to hear. "You found something?"

Theo nodded.

"What?"

Theo jerked his head, indicating that they should follow.

"Gosh, I wish he'd shut up once in a while," Abby said from behind Sam, just loud enough for Sam and no one else to hear.

Sam grinned. They followed Theo around the bend in the river to see . . . tourists!

Three bright-green vans were parked on a gravel patch next to the river, and yellow inflatable rafts had been laid out by the water. People were milling around, putting on life jackets and helmets, picking up oars, listening to guides who were shouting directions.

Sam was startled, but really, it shouldn't have been such a surprise. This was a hugely popular national park, after all. All sorts of people came here. They'd been riding and walking alone for hours, and he'd begun to feel as if they were as isolated as Lewis and Clark's men had been two centuries ago. But that wasn't true, and a good thing too.

Theo looked back. The four of them gathered close together by the riverbank. Sam could see by the looks on their faces that they all had the same idea.

"Swim with the current?" Sam asked. The other three nodded.

"We've just got to look like we're part of the group," Marty said. "Come on!"

They quickly made their way to the spot where the vans had been parked. Everyone was too busy with their preparations to notice four extra kids who wandered out casually from behind a van, trying hard to look as if they'd been there all along. Once Theo picked up life jackets from a pile on the ground and they'd all pulled them on, they looked just like the other tourists, ready for action.

"Wow," said a voice from near the ground, and Sam looked down to see a little girl gazing up at Theo. She had another little girl by the hand, and they looked like a duplicated picture—same blond ponytails, same pink T-shirts, same looks of awe. "You're tall."

Theo looked a little confused. "Yes. I guess. I am." He looked as if he hoped that would be the end of it.

"Can we go in your raft?" the first girl asked. Sam was stifling a smile. Theo was looking seriously panicked. "I want to go with you. My sister does too. She's four. I'm four too."

"Uh, I don't think so," Theo answered. Both girls' faces sank. The talkative one looked tragic.

"Don't you have . . . parents?" Theo looked around, spotted Sam's grin, and gave him a "you're dead when I have time to bother" look.

"You're a chick magnet," Sam told him.

Theo threatened him with a paddle, and a cheerful-looking woman in a floppy cloth hat came up to pull the girls away and zip on their life jackets.

"Listen up!" one of the guides was shouting, a short, sunburned man with a scruffy beard and a ponytail. He was wearing a wetsuit that looked like it had been through a mangle. Sam eyed a rip along one forearm a little nervously. "Four in a raft, people. Grab your paddles and strap on your helmets. Stick close to the raft in front of you. This is a gentle stretch of the river, and there hasn't been a lot of rain recently, so it's not going to be too fast—but you can never be too careful. Let's go!"

The four kids hung back and snagged the last raft in line, climbing in awkwardly. Marty sat in front of Sam on one side, fastening a helmet strap under her chin. Theo was behind Abby on the other.

"Have you done this before?" Marty shouted at Theo as a guide, a young woman with more muscles in her arms than Sam had in his entire body, shoved their raft out into the current.

"No! You?"

"Abby!" Marty yelled. "Tell me you've done this! I am not even thinking of counting on Sam!"

"A few times!" Abby called as their raft gently rotated in the water, giving them a spectacular view of the river valley but leaving them moving along backward. "Um . . . Sam and Marty, don't do anything. Theo, you paddle now." His paddle clashed with hers just above the surface of the water, and the raft wobbled. "Oops! Wait a second. One, two, three. Now! That should spin us around. There!"

She was right. Their raft came around so they were facing the right way, to the giggles of some of the other rafters. The guide who'd pushed them into the water had jumped into a small kayak and now zipped up behind them, as comfortable in the water as Sam would be on a skateboard.

"Hold your paddles like this!" she called out over the noise of the water. "See?" She showed them how to get the most power out of their strokes, and nodded as they began to move more quickly through the water. "The current will carry you!" she called out. "All you need to do is steer a bit. Don't worry. You'll have fun!" She darted away to help the family with the twin girls. The four kids came up behind the other rafters just in time for Marty to get a face full of water, shot from the paddle of a pudgy boy in the raft in front of them.

"You did that on purpose!" she spluttered, trying helplessly to wipe her wet glasses with her wetter hands.

"Did not!" The boy stuck his tongue out, and when his parents were not looking, splashed her again. Abby deftly slipped her paddle forward and gave him a thorough dunking.

"Young lady, watch what you're doing!" one of the adults in the other raft called out sternly.

"Sorry!" Abby said serenely as they all leaned into their paddles, passing that raft and then a few more until they were in the center of the group.

This wasn't bad, Sam thought. The water splashing up from the river was cold, but the sun warmed his shoulders and back through his life jacket. He pulled the compass out of his pocket to check the direction. They were heading the right way, and much, much faster than they could have done walking. Also, Sam thought, much more comfortably than it would have been if he'd had to keep on sitting on a horse.

"White water up ahead!" Abby called.

Maybe Sam had gotten comfortable a little too soon . . .

The current quickened beneath them as the river narrowed. One of the twin girls squealed as her raft slid over a boulder hidden beneath the surface. Little waves began to seethe and boil around Sam's raft as the bottom got rockier.

"Work together!" called out the guide in the kayak. "People in the front, call out directions!"

"Left!" Abby shouted. "Sam and Marty, paddle on the left!"

They did as she said and swept past a giant gray boulder sticking up out of the water, slick and wet with spray. The raft was acting like Snickers now, bouncing up and down beneath Sam, and he shoved his feet under a strap for stability, hanging on tight to his paddle.

"Two big boulders coming up!" Abby called back. "We'll have to go between them. Sam and Marty, paddle on the left again. Good!"

Peering over Marty's shoulder, Sam could see the two boulders Abby had been talking about. They were huge! The size of cars, they huddled in the middle of the river, and the water poured between them, white and churning with speed.

"Theo, you and me now. Just one stroke. There!" Abby kept coaching them. "It's coming up. Paddles out of the water. Just let the current take us . . . go!"

They went. The current seized their raft and swept it between the rocks, fast as a roller coaster—at least it felt that way to Sam. Walls of gray rock swept past his face as his heart thumped heavily under his life jacket. Spray showered him, and then they were through!

The river widened out at once, and they paddled quickly into the calmer water, letting rafters behind them shoot between the boulders as well. The boy who'd splashed Marty shrieked with terror and dropped his paddle. One of the guides had to go retrieve it.

"Hey, we did it. We're through!" Sam grinned. The river was smooth underneath them now, and they could drift easily on the current. "We're a team. Way to go! Hey, Marty, high-five me. No, with your paddle!"

"Really, Sam?" Marty sighed but held out her paddle to one side so Sam could slap it with his. When she looked back at him, she was smiling, blinking at him through glasses misted with spray.

"Are we still on course?" she asked him.

"Let me check." He got the compass out of his pocket and held it out. "Yeah . . . kind of."

"What does 'kind of' mean?" Marty asked.

"We're going roughly the right direction. But the needle's pointing a bit more that way—" He pointed to the right with his paddle. "And the river's headed straight."

"Everybody over to the left!" called back the pony-tailed guide from the front raft. "The river's about to fork, and I want you all over here. Left, please!"

"But we don't want to go left." Marty twisted around to share a quick glance with them all. "When the river forks, we'd better go right."

Sam nodded. "We can't let anybody see us, though. Drop back to the end of the line."

They slowed down, letting raft after raft pass them until they were the last except for one person—the guide in the kayak.

And no matter how much they slowed down, she stayed behind them. It was clearly her job to stay in the back, making sure nobody ran aground or went astray. How could they get away without her seeing them?

"There's the fork, coming up," Abby called back softly. Sam leaned around Marty again and saw the river split around a rocky outcrop with a few scrubby, gnarled pine trees clinging to shallow drifts of soil.

"I dropped my paddle! I'm wet! I don't *like* this vacation!" came a wailing voice from up ahead. It was the boy who'd splashed Marty. The guide in the kayak sprinted ahead to pick up the paddle again. Sam distinctly heard her sigh as she went past their raft.

"This is our chance—let's go!" Abby called in a low voice.

Behind the guide, out of her sight, they leaned into their paddles and drove the raft toward the right side of the river. The current picked up speed beneath them, and in a few minutes the rocky point of land cut them off from the rest of the rafters. They were out of sight and once again on their own.

"Smooth move!" Sam rested his paddle on his knees. No point in working hard now. The current was carrying them along nicely.

In fact, the current was speeding up. The river was narrowing, the sides becoming rockier and steeper, sloping down to the swiftly moving water.

"Maybe we should try to slow down." Marty's voice sounded anxious. "I can't see what's ahead."

Sam peered around her shoulder once more, only to see the river disappear around the bend. "It's not like we can hit the brakes, Marty. Don't sweat it. Didn't we handle those rapids all right?"

"No, she's right." Abby's voice was sharp. "Back paddle! Everybody!"

"Do what now?" Sam shouted. It was getting harder to hear what anybody was saying.

"Paddle backward!" Abby shouted. "Hard! Now!" And then she added something that Sam couldn't catch, something that started with "Can't you hear—"

But all that Sam could hear was the river getting louder and louder. He dug in with his paddle, trying to slow the raft, as Theo and Marty and Abby did the same. The muscles in his arms and shoulders strained, but it was like digging into frozen ground. No matter how hard he tried, it did no good at all.

The current swept them around a bend, and then another. The raft plowed through a cloud of white spray, bounced off a boulder, and spun madly as it sprang back into the current. Riverbank, bright sky, and rushing water flashed past as they turned. Then Sam caught a glimpse of what lay downstream, and his heart leaped into his throat. Just ahead, the entire river poured right over a cliff.

"Paddle!" Abby shrieked. "As hard as you can!"

But it was no use. The relentless current had them. For a moment, the raft seemed to hang at the edge of the waterfall, as if gravity had somehow been canceled just for them. Sam's entire body turned icy with terror.

Then they fell.

CHAPTER SIX

The raft plunged downward, in free fall along with the water around it. Sam could hear somebody screaming.

Maybe he was the one screaming.

Even worse than the sickening fall was the endless second he had to anticipate hitting the pool at the bottom of the waterfall.

Then they hit, slamming into water that felt as hard as concrete. Sam, along with his friends, was bounced out of the raft like popcorn bouncing off a hot skillet. He snatched in a breath before freezing, angry water yanked him under.

Swimming wasn't even a possibility. He thrashed and kicked, but it made no difference to the current, which swirled him in a circle, let him up briefly to breathe, pulled him under again, and then spit him out so he drifted help-lessly into the calmer shallows.

His rib cage thumped into something solid and smooth—a rock! He seized hold, crawled up onto the solid surface, and lay flat, dripping water and heaving in gulps of air.

Marty had her own rock. Abby had crawled out onto a little stony beach, littered with driftwood and clumps of dead leaves. Theo was standing near her, knee-deep in the swirling water, watching their raft disappear far down-stream.

"I am never," Sam said shakily, and coughed, and sat up shivering, "going on a log flume ride ever again."

Abby giggled very faintly. Marty gave Sam an impa-tient look, climbed off her rock, and sloshed over to join Abby and Theo on the beach. Sam followed.

"Sam! Get that!" Abby called out.

"Get what?" Sam asked.

"That pack!"

Sam looked around. His pack, which had been tossed out of the raft, had washed up in the water near his feet. He snagged it, and then saw Marty's as well—it was bigger and heavier than anybody else's. He got that too, dragging both to the shore. There was no sign of Abby's pack, though, or Theo's. They must have been washed downstream or sunk into the churning pool beneath the waterfall.

"Well," Abby said. She propped herself against a dead tree, pulled off her helmet, and started wringing water out of her hair. "I guess we know why the guides didn't want us to take this fork of the river."

"No kidding." Sam took off his helmet too, then pulled off his boots and dumped water out of them. The sun was beginning to warm him up a little. "So what now?"

"Is the compass okay, Sam?" Marty asked.

The compass! Sam hadn't even thought about it. But surely the antique mechanism wasn't made to be thrown over a waterfall and dunked in freezing water. He scrabbled at his pocket to get it out and sighed with relief to see that it hadn't gotten smashed.

"It's okay." He shook the compass a little to make sure no water was sloshing around inside. "Or—uh. Maybe not."

"What's wrong with it?" In a moment, Marty was on her knees at his side. Theo looked over their shoulders, and Abby also came to see.

"The needle," Sam said, staring in confusion. Every other time he'd looked at the compass, the needle had quivered for a moment and then pointed firmly northeast. But it wasn't doing that anymore. It wobbled a little and then it pointed firmly south, across the river.

"It's changed," he said, baffled.

"It can't have." Marty was frowning down at the compass. "A compass doesn't change, not like that. It can only point in one direction."

"Well, this one did." Sam handed her the compass—maybe staring at the quivering needle would make her feel better, but all it was doing to Sam was making him nauseated. Or maybe it was their situation that was creating that queasy churning inside him.

They were in the middle of a wilderness with no horses, no raft, only two packs, and no easy way out. And Thomas Jefferson's compass wanted them to trek off to the south now? How were they supposed to do that? When he looked to the other side of the river, he saw nothing but endless rows of dense trees, a solid wall of green. Could the four of them really bushwhack their way through that?

And what would happen if Gideon Arnold got tired of waiting?

Sam didn't want to think about that.

He looked around. They'd followed the compass this far, trusting that it was a clue from Thomas Jefferson. They'd done just what the thing said—literally, in fact. They had swum with the current.

"In matters of style, swim with the current," Sam muttered to himself, trying to see if saying the words out loud would turn up any new ideas. "In matters of principle, stand like a rock."

Like a rock . . .

Or *on* a rock?

Sam stood up, grabbed the compass from Marty, and plunged right back into the water. "I was sitting on it!" Sam yelled, and suddenly he felt like laughing. "The whole time! I guess I should have stood on it instead! Maybe then I would have seen it!"

"He gets like this sometimes." Marty sighed as she got to her feet. "What are you talking about, Sam? Please remember that the rest of us can't join you in the strange and frightening place that is the inside of your head."

"Come and look at this!" Standing knee deep in swirling water, Sam slapped the rock that he'd been washed up on. He'd been so grateful to breathe at last that he hadn't even looked at it.

Or at what was carved on its surface.

Theo, Marty, and Abby all waded out into the pool. Water swirled around their knees as they studied what Sam had found—a pyramid with a quill in its center, cut into the rock. Water and wind had rubbed away at the lines, but they were still there.

Jefferson's pyramid. It was a clue, the next clue! Falling over that waterfall had not been a disaster after all. It had brought them right where they'd needed to be!

"Look at the compass," Marty said, grabbing Sam's wrist. She pulled his hand with the compass in it closer to her eyes. "If we stand on this rock and look at the compass, maybe that'll be our next clue—oh. No."

Sam looked down at the compass as well, and saw what Marty was seeing. The needle now swung in wide, wobbling circles, as if it had no idea anymore which way they should go.

"I guess the compass was just supposed to get us here," Sam said. "To this rock. Now it's not going to help us anymore."

"So what are we supposed to do next?" Abby asked, looking around as if the trees or the clouds would toss down an idea.

"Figure out our next clue," Sam said. "This rock. What's it telling us?"

"Look at the pyramid," Marty said. "It's not like the other Founders' pyramids I've seen."

"You're right." Theo rolled up his sleeve to compare the pyramid on the rock to the one tattooed on his forearm.

The pyramid on the rock was much narrower than the one on Theo's skin. It was almost as if somebody had grabbed the tip and pulled, making it longer and skinnier.

"That's strange," Theo said. "The Founders' symbol is always the same. I've never seen it look like that."

"It doesn't look so much like a pyramid at all, really," Sam said, feeling a thought take shape inside his head. The apex of the pyramid, the part with the eye, was pointing upstream.

"Does it look anything like an arrow to you guys?" Sam turned to look. "An arrow pointing . . ." He let his voice trail off.

"At the waterfall?" Abby's voice rose with disbelief. "The waterfall is our next clue?"

"Maybe not the waterfall itself," Marty said. "Maybe something . . . behind it?"

"A cave," Sam said, nodding. "Something underground. Like that old mine in Death Valley. Those Founders really loved deep, dark, scary places."

Theo was already sloshing back toward the beach. The little curving shelf of gravel and driftwood extended all the way around the pool beneath the waterfall. The others followed Theo, only getting as far as the beach by the time Theo was right next to the curtain of thundering white water.

Two or three feet above Theo's head, a small ledge jutted out from the cliff face. The waterfall poured over it, leaving a small gap between the powerful, rushing water and the rocky wall.

Cautiously, Theo flattened himself against the cliff and stepped into this gap. He took another step and disappeared.

Sam held his breath. Two seconds later, Theo was out again, shaking his head and spraying water all around. He waved at them to come with him and vanished behind the waterfall again.

Sam picked up his pack, Marty took hers, and they all followed Theo behind the water and into what lay beyond.

The waterfall cut out the light once they had stepped through it. "Hold on," came Marty's voice from a patch of darkness to Sam's left. "I've got a flashlight, a waterproof one."

"Of course you do," Sam said, digging in his pack for his own light.

"Are you complaining, Sam?" A brilliant white beam sliced through the darkness and landed on Sam's face.

"Uh, nope. Not at all." Sam pulled out his flashlight and looked at it in dismay. "Especially because mine's toast," he added, shaking broken glass from his flashlight's shattered lens out onto the cave's floor. "But turn that thing somewhere else, would you, Marty?"

Marty did, and the flashlight's beam bounced off rough gray walls, a floor slick with mud, and a lumpy ceiling that nearly brushed Theo's head.

"What's that smell?" When the light touched Abby's face, Sam saw that she was wrinkling her nose.

Sam sniffed and winced. "The third-floor boys' bathroom at my school?"

"Disgusting," Marty said. "So what are we supposed to do now? Is there another arrow or something to show us the way?"

There wasn't. But that was probably simply because there was only one way they *could* go. The narrow cave headed straight back into the cliff, a passageway that stretched far beyond the reach of Marty's flashlight.

"Let's go," Theo said. "Marty, take the light and go in front. Stay close together, everybody."

"You got that right," Abby agreed, falling into step behind Sam as he followed Theo. Her voice was a little jumpy, and Sam glanced back at her, seeing her wide eyes and tense mouth in the light that reflected off the rock walls all around them.

He shot her what he hoped was a reassuring grin. "Hey, listen. It's not as bad as that abandoned mine in Death Valley. Did I tell you about that? And that crazy sundial that was set up to fry anybody who couldn't figure out the puzzle? At least this time all we had to do was fall down a water—*ah!*"

Sam had stepped on something that rolled beneath his foot. He staggered, trying to keep his balance, bounced off Theo, rebounded into a wall, and ended up sitting in a mud puddle on the ground.

"Sam? What's wrong?" Marty swept the light around.

"I stepped on—*ah!*" Sam yelled again and scrambled to his feet. "That! I stepped on that!"

It was a bone. Long and skinny, it looked like it had once been part of somebody's leg. And there were marks on it.

Sam bent closer, swallowing a surge of nausea. Tooth marks. The bone had been chewed on by . . . by . . . by he didn't know what. By something with really big teeth.

"Oh no . . . ," Abby whispered.

"I don't think I like this direction after all." Sam took a few jittery steps back toward the cave's entrance. "It looks like the last person who made it here didn't get any farther. Actually, it looks like a lot of people didn't get any farther." His eyes widened as Marty let the light play across the cave floor. Rib bones curved up from the ground. Leg bones were scattered in piles.

Theo made an odd sound and reached out to put a hand against the wall.

"Theo? You all right?" Sam took a step toward him and accidentally kicked a pile of vertebrae, sending them bouncing over the stone floor. "Sorry!" he muttered, in case whoever these bones belonged to were hanging around to haunt the cave and didn't appreciate having their remains used for soccer practice.

"Look at this!" Marty straightened up, holding something big and white in her hands.

"Marty! You really think you should pick those things up?" Sam was getting the creeps. He'd seen enough horror movies to know that it was a really, really bad idea to hang around a pile of gnawed-up bones. "We should be getting out of here!"

"Sam, *look*. For Pete's sake!" Marty held out her bone. It had eerily empty eye sockets, a long, skinny face, and two horns branching off its forehead. "It's a mountain goat skull. All of these are animal bones."

"You're sure?" Theo asked a little hoarsely.

"Of course I'm sure. For one thing, people don't have horns." Marty tossed the skull back down. "Everybody relax."

"I'm not so sure that's a good idea," Abby said.

"Why?" Sam turned to look at her.

"Because—"

But Marty interrupted her. "Theo? What's the matter?"

Theo had found something among the tangle of bones. He reached down slowly to pick it up, and Sam forgot to wonder what Abby had been going to say when he saw the look on Theo's face.

"Theo?" He kicked his way through more goat bones to the big guy's side. "What's that?"

"A pack," Theo answered. It hung limply from his hands, a sagging pouch of dark-blue nylon. "Empty. Except—"

From a small, zippered pocket, he pulled out a necklace. It glinted in the beam of Marty's flashlight, a twirling silver pendant on an intricate chain. A triangular pendant. Sam put a hand out to stop the thing from twirling and held it still. On one side, etched into the silver was a pyramid with a sword inside. On the other side were two initials—*C* and *W*.

Holding the pendant, Theo stood without moving, even his fingers frozen. But his breath came out in a long, low sigh.

"Theo?" Marty gently pushed Sam's hand away from the pendant. "That's your Founders' symbol, the one that's tattooed on your arm. Were you expecting to find it here?"

She'd noticed the same thing Sam had noticed—that Theo didn't look happy to see the pendant, but he also didn't look surprised.

"What's going on?" Marty asked. "What aren't you telling us?"

The pendant twisted gently, and the silence seemed to stretch out endlessly. Just when Sam thought he was about to scream with frustration, Theo spoke.

"It's my mom's," he said, and suddenly bunched his fist around the pendant and shoved it into a pocket.

"Your mom was here?" Sam looked around, as if he might see a female version of Theo—tall, strong, and in charge—stepping out of the shadows.

"I guess she was," Theo said flatly.

"Tell us, Theo." Marty's voice was gentle.

Theo took in a slow breath and nodded. "You remember Evangeline said that one of her *associates* tried to check on the artifacts? That was my mom. We know she was headed here, to Glacier Park. But two months ago, we stopped hearing from her."

"And you didn't come after her?" Sam asked, startled. Theo turned on him so quickly Sam had to fight the urge to take a step backward.

"I wanted to! But Evangeline said no. She and my mom were good friends, really good. I was staying with Evangeline while my mom was gone. Evangeline kept saying we should trust my mom, that she'd be back. Because she wouldn't have—"

"Wouldn't have what?" Sam asked, a little warily.

Theo rubbed at the inside of his left arm, where his tattoo lay hidden under his shirt. "Wouldn't have left without telling me where to find Washington's vault. If she thought there'd be any danger. If she actually thought she might—die."

They all stared at the empty pack, shaken.

"Well." Sam hesitated, then spoke. "So maybe Evangeline was right, Theo."

"Right?" Theo suddenly crumbled up the empty pack and let it drop from his hands. "I should have come to look for her!"

"Theo, listen!" Sam raised his voice. "Her things are gone, right? The pack's empty?"

"So?"

"So she took her stuff. The point is, she didn't just drop the pack and run. She had a plan."

Theo looked a little startled, but then shook his head. "Or somebody else took her things after she . . ."

"Theo. Man. Don't go there."

Theo was still shaking his head. "She wouldn't have left the necklace. She never would have done that, if she'd had a choice."

"Oh." Sam sagged. His attempt at comforting Theo had fallen apart.

"Theo." Abby sniffed hard. Her eyes were shiny in the dim light, and Sam realized she was about to cry. "I know how you feel. You know I do. My parents . . ." She took a quick breath and went on. "But we can't give up hope, not now. We've got to keep going."

"She's right," Marty said, patting Theo's arm. "Theo, I'm so sorry. But you can't believe the worst, not without proof."

Sam even jumped in to try again. "If your mom's anything like you, Theo, she's as tough as nails. I wouldn't give up on her. If she's alive, we'll find her."

Theo stared down at the crumpled pack at his feet, and then slowly bent to retrieve it. He slung it on his back, looked around at all his friends, and nodded once.

"Let's keep going," he said hoarsely.

"We'd better," Abby said. "I didn't want to say, but those bones—something brings its prey here to eat. And we don't want to be hanging around when it—"

"Comes back?" Marty said. Her voice quavered.

"Right," Abby said, and looked in surprise at Marty's pale face. "Marty? What's up?"

Marty pointed the flashlight down the way they had come, and the light bounced off rock walls and ceiling as her hand trembled. "I saw something back there. Just for a second . . ."

"What? What did you see?" Sam asked.

"Eyes."

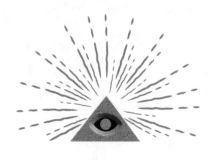

Chapter Seven

"Eyes!" Sam leaped to Marty's side as she stood, playing the light back down the cave. "What kind of eyes? How big? How, you know, evil?"

"Sam, shut up! They were pretty big. And kind of yellow. They flashed like a cat's eyes in the dark. But I don't see anything now . . ."

"Like a cat?" Abby said sharply.

"Yes. But way too big to be a cat . . ."

"Maybe too big for a housecat," Theo muttered. "But they've got other kinds of cats around here."

"We've got to go." Abby began backing up farther into the cave. "Come on!"

"Why?" Sam followed her, happy to be away from creepy flashing yellow eyes but wanting to know more. "What do you think it is?"

"A mountain lion, probably," Abby answered. "Theo, Marty, come on! Get away from the bones. That's its cache, where it brings its prey to eat. A mountain lion will kill anything it thinks might be after its food. No, Marty, don't run!"

"Don't run! Why not?" Marty demanded.

"Because cats chase things that run. Haven't you ever seen one go after a mouse?"

Marty gulped back a little whimpering sound and slowed down. "So what do we do?"

"We walk," Abby said grimly, reaching out to grab Marty's arm and pull her close. "And we stay close together. And we hope it isn't hungry."

Sam crowded close to Abby and Marty, with Theo in the lead as they pressed farther back into the cave. Sam could hear nothing except their scuffling footfalls and their tense breathing. But you wouldn't expect to hear a hunting cat, would you? A cat that was a noisy hunter would be a cat that starved to death pretty quickly.

On either side the walls were narrowing, closing in, and soon they were forced to walk single file. Sam began to worry that they were headed into a dead end, and a dead end right now could be very dead indeed. Were they just setting themselves up to be a nice little cat buffet? Behind Sam, last in line, Marty swung the light back and forth, trying to light up the path in front of them as well as turning around to scan the cave for the big cat behind.

"It's probably scared of the light," Abby said softly. "Maybe we can . . ." She reached down and snatched up a leg bone from the litter at their feet.

"Abby? What are you doing?" Sam asked.

"Give me something from your pack," Abby said, her eyes on the darkness behind them. "Something that will burn."

They stopped walking, huddling close together. Theo bent down to pick up a leg bone as well, with a hoof still attached. Marty kept the flashlight's beam moving, but as the light shifted from damp wall to rough ceiling to muddy floor, it cast thick black shadows behind piles of boulders and lumps of stone, shadows where almost anything could be hiding.

Including a cat the size of a Saint Bernard.

Sam dug in his pack, finding a waterproof bag that he'd stuffed with what few clothes he had left that hadn't been lost or taken by Arnold's men. He yanked out a sweatshirt and groaned a little as he handed it to Abby.

"What?" she asked.

"It's my best Wolverine one," he told her.

"Priorities, Sam!" Marty snapped while Abby ruthlessly ripped Sam's favorite sweatshirt into three or four wide strips, twisting them around the bone.

She snapped her fingers. "Matches!"

"Hurry," Theo said in a low voice.

"Why?" Sam asked.

"Because I just saw that shadow move."

"Which shadow?" Sam asked, his voice jumping with nerves. Then he saw for himself. Behind a huge boulder, a dark, curling line lay along the stone floor. It twitched.

Sam had watched his neighbor's cat stalk a bird once. It had flattened itself in the grass and lay so still, you might have thought it was a garden ornament—except that every now and then, the very tip of its tail jerked with excitement.

Sam had thrown an acorn to startle the bird into flight, and the cat had glared at him and stalked away. Nobody was going to save the four of them by throwing an acorn now.

"Matches!" Abby said again, and Sam snapped his eyes away from the darkness behind the rock and dug into his pack. He'd packed matches, he knew he had . . . but he didn't know where he had put them. He rooted through Snickers bars, bags of M&M's, a soggy fleece jacket, a bottle of bug spray, another of water . . .

"Watch out!" Theo yelled, and Sam looked up.

In one smooth and sudden movement, a huge cat—it looked as big as a car to Sam—flung itself up over the shelter of the boulder. It was a tawny blur in the air with eyes that caught the flashlight's beam in a blaze of fiery gold.

They all cried out in shock. Sam felt his heart thud against his ribs, and then it seemed to stop beating entirely. Or maybe it was time that had stopped. There was a moment where the mountain lion seemed to hang in mid-air, claws out, forelegs wide. Sam could see the cat's red mouth and its sharp, curved, ivory teeth.

Then Theo stepped forward and braced himself like a major league batter facing a pitcher with a wicked fast-ball. He swung his length of bone. It hit the mountain lion in the face, and the animal yowled, flung off balance. It twisted in the air to land on three feet, keeping its left front leg off the ground.

"Matches! Now!" Abby shrieked.

Sam snapped his attention back to his pack. With the flashlight trembling in her left hand, Marty grabbed up a skull and threw it with her right. The cat dodged, snarling with rage. Sam snagged a waterproof plastic pouch and fum-bled it open. Abby snatched the matches from his hands.

The cat crouched low to the ground, its tail lashing angrily against the floor. It still kept one front paw up off the ground, as if it didn't want to put weight on it, and opened its mouth wide to let out a deafening hiss of frus-tration. It didn't seem to know what to do with prey that fought back, but it wasn't going to retreat either.

Abby struck a match, dropped it, struck a second, and held its flame to the edge of one of the soft rags she'd twisted around her bone. In a moment flames were blossoming on her makeshift torch.

She leaned past Theo to shove the torch at the mountain lion. It hissed again and backed away.

"Let's go," Abby said, her voice quavering.

They hurried farther into the cave, Abby now walking backward at the end of the line, brandishing her torch. Sam took hold of her arm to guide her. The mountain lion snarled, a sound that rumbled off the stone walls like faraway, drawn-out thunder, but it didn't follow.

The walls closed in tighter. They were in more of a tunnel than a cave now, going deeper and deeper into the heart of the cliff.

The tunnel twisted, and they lost sight of the mountain lion. "Now it can't see us," Abby said. "Better run. This torch won't keep burning forever!"

They followed her advice, their feet thudding against the floor of the cave. The tunnel stretched out before them, mostly level, twisting and turning till Sam had no idea which way they were going. How many minutes had they been running? Three? Fifteen? It was hard to be sure. In front, Marty's flashlight beam bounced off shiny walls, dripping with water. The ground seemed to be getting wetter under Sam's feet; drops splashed down from the ceiling onto his head and neck. One hit the torch and the flames sizzled and spat.

"Watch out!" Marty called. "We're going downhill!"
She was right. In a moment, the ground under Sam's feet
sloped downward. His feet skidded through mud and
gravel. Then Marty yelled.

"Stop! Stop!"

Sam grabbed at the walls, trying to slow his pace, and
his feet went out from under him. He crashed into Theo,
who fell on top of him, and the two of them slid into
Marty, who threw herself to one side, rolling away.

Sam and Theo, in a tangle, slid to a halt. "Ow," Sam
muttered. His elbows were stinging, his back was aching,
and it was extremely hard to breathe with Theo squashing
him. The older boy rolled off, and Sam saw for the first
time why Marty had yelled.

They had just slid into an immense cave, cut through
the middle by a deep ravine. Theo's feet were only a few
inches from its edge.

"When I said 'stop' I didn't mean 'knock me down'!"
Marty said, picking herself up as Abby came up from
behind them, her torch still flickering in her hand. Theo
and Sam inched back from the ravine's edge before getting
to their feet, and Sam took a look around, trying to figure
out where they'd ended up.

The cave rose up all around them, and it looked
bigger than a football stadium to Sam. Faint light from
Marty's flashlight bounced off an arching ceiling that

dripped with stalactites. The ravine cut through the cave from edge to edge, and the beam of light could only make a feeble attempt to pierce the darkness inside it. Sam could not see the bottom, but somewhere, deep down, he could hear quickly moving water thundering against stone walls.

"So what do we do now?" he asked, shivering a little. "Jump across?" He rubbed his arms, because it was cold down here and his sweatshirt was currently smoldering, wrapped around the leg bone of a mountain goat. Not because he'd come close to sliding into a bottomless pit. Of course not.

"We don't have to jump," Marty said.

"You're planning to fly?"

"I'm planning to walk on the bridge." Marty pointed her flashlight to their right, along the edge of the ravine, and Sam saw what she meant. It was the weirdest-looking bridge he had ever seen.

In fact, it was two bridges—sort of. Two wooden planks, each about the width of a sidewalk, reached from edge to edge of the ravine. A thick wooden pole stood between them, with a beam across it, making a *T* shape. The planks had been suspended from the beam by a system of rigid metal cables. Above the bridge, there seemed to be some sort of crack that reached up to the surface, because dim sunlight spilled down through the damp air.

The four kids walked cautiously along the edge of the ravine to the bridge. "It looks kind of familiar," Marty said, frowning and pushing her glasses up a little bit on her nose.

"They have some pretty weird bridges where you're from, huh?" Sam picked up a small stone from near his foot and pitched in into the murk. There was an extremely long pause before he heard the faintest possible splash.

"No." Marty let her light play over the planks, the central supporting beam, the walls of the pit. "That's not why. It reminds me of something . . . oh!"

She stopped. The beam of the flashlight had caught something on the far wall of the ravine—letters. She moved the light along. Carved into the stone of the ravine was the phrase "All men are created equal."

"From the Declaration of Independence," Marty said.

"We do know that, Marty. We're not complete morons," Sam told her.

"But Thomas Jefferson *wrote* that, Sam! It proves we're on the right track. This is the next clue!"

"Of course it is," Sam said. "Obviously. It's a crazy bridge over a bottomless pit in the middle of the wilderness. Only a Founder would build something like this." He sighed. "And I guess we've got to cross it."

"Your other choice is to go back and see if that mountain lion is still looking for a snack," Marty told him.

"No thanks." Sam took a closer look at the bridge. The planks, he saw, did not actually reach from side to side of the ravine, as he had thought at first. There was a gap of at least a foot between each plank and the rocky edge of the ravine.

"It doesn't look very sturdy," Theo remarked, craning his neck to peer over the edge of the precipice.

"Maybe the ravine's eroded some since the bridge was first built," Marty said, noticing the same thing. "It seems okay, though. We can still use it."

"If you say so," Abby said. "You first."

"Fine with me!" Marty huffed. She drew in a deep breath and then took a step across the gap, getting first one foot and then the other on the left-hand plank. "See? Not too bad!" She looked back over her shoulder. "Come on, who's next?"

The plank began to tip under her feet.

It wasn't just the plank that was moving, in fact. The entire *bridge* was tipping to the left, rocking on the central support beam. Marty's weight had pulled it out of balance, and the right-hand plank was coming up while Marty's plank went down.

"Marty! Get off that thing!" Theo yelled.

Sam threw himself forward as Marty shrieked and whipped around, windmilling her arms. Her heavy pack pulled her off balance. Before she could jump, she fell.

Sam crashed to his knees at the edge of the ravine and threw himself flat on his stomach, grabbing for Marty as her body thumped into the rocks of the ravine's wall. His left hand got a handful of damp fleece jacket; his right got her left wrist. For a moment he supported all her weight, and he wasn't sure if he could hold on. Then Theo was beside him, reaching out to seize hold of Marty's arms as well, and the burden on Sam's muscles eased.

"Marty! You okay?" Sam asked.

"I am so not okay!" Marty looked up into their faces as she dangled above endless blackness. Behind her, the bridge began slowly righting itself, the planks returning to level. "Pull me up!"

"See if you can brace your feet on the rocks," Theo told her. "Okay, Sam, on three. One . . . two . . ."

Behind them, Abby shrieked.

Still holding tight to Marty, Sam twisted around. Abby was facing the way they had come, swinging her feebly flickering torch through the air. Sam heard a growl, low enough to vibrate in his chest and make the skin along his back crawl with horror.

In the darkness where the tunnel met the cave, eyes flashed gold.

"The torch is going out!" Abby yelled.

"Sam! Keep hold of Marty!" Theo said urgently and let go.

Sam wanted to say something sarcastic to Theo—"Well, I *was* planning to drop her to her death, but since you said not to . . ." But all he had breath to do was grunt as Marty's full weight swung from his hands once again.

"Sam!" she gasped, and her eyes were wide and frightened behind her glasses.

"Don't . . . worry . . ." Sam got out between gritted teeth.

He didn't have any idea what was going on behind his back now. He couldn't turn his head to see. He heard Abby gasp, and then a thump, and another, and an angry hiss from the big cat.

With her left hand, the one Theo had dropped, Marty grabbed a rocky outcrop. She scrabbled with her feet at the ravine's side and got a bit of her weight on a ledge only an inch or two wide.

"Good," Sam muttered. "Come on. Up you come . . ."

The mountain lion yowled behind Sam. "Good shot!" Abby shouted.

Sam ordered all the strength he could summon into his shoulders and arms, and slowly, steadily, lifted Marty an inch. Another. She set her teeth and pulled at the rocks with her free hand, hoisting herself up farther. On his stomach, Sam writhed backward along the cave floor, dragging Marty with him. His muscles burned. His chin scraped against the ground.

The little spur of rock Marty was holding onto crumbled in her hands. With a sharp cry, she slid back, and her weight dragged Sam forward too. He tried to brace himself against the stones, but it wasn't any use. He was sliding. Marty's face was close to his, and her look of terror mirrored the one he could feel on his own face.

Then Theo was on his knees beside them again, leaning over to grab Marty's shoulders. "Now!" he shouted, and Sam heaved, and between them they hauled Marty onto the wet, muddy stone floor.

Panting, Sam shoved himself up into a sitting position. "Where's the mountain lion?" he wheezed.

"It backed off into the tunnel. Theo hit it with a couple of rocks," Abby said, coming to kneel beside Marty. She laid the burned-out torch down on the ground and patted Marty's shoulders. "Are you okay?" Marty nodded, shaking, her mouth tight. It looked to Sam as if she were trying hard not to let herself cry.

"You're not hurt, are you, Marty?" Sam peered at her closely.

She shook her head. "Just . . ." Her voice trailed off.

"You are so brave," Abby said with admiration gleaming in her eyes. "I can't believe what you did! Stepping onto the bridge like that."

Marty blinked at Abby, looking a little surprised. She stopped shivering.

"We should have known it wouldn't be that easy," Sam said, shaking his head. "It's a Founder thing. It's a puzzle." He sighed. "It's always a puzzle."

"Then we'd better solve it quick," Abby said. "That lion might be back any minute. Did you see it limping? It's hurt. Probably it hasn't been able to hunt. It's hungry."

Sam shuddered. "That isn't exactly helping me think!" He stared hard at the bridge. They couldn't just step out onto it—Marty had proved that. It would tip with any weight. But nobody built a bridge that couldn't be crossed either. There had to be a way.

"All men are created equal," Marty said suddenly, confidence back in her voice. "Equal!" She slapped Sam's shoulder, and he jumped.

"What? Don't hit me!"

"I knew the bridge looked familiar!" Marty said. "It looks like a scale, don't you see? It *is* a scale. Like the Scale of Justice!"

Sam knew what she meant—the blindfolded figure of Justice herself, holding a perfectly balanced scale. "Yeah. Yeah, you're right. So if the weights are *equal*, just like Thomas Jefferson said—"

"Then the bridge won't tip!" Marty finished for him.

"So two people have to cross together. One on each plank." Sam jumped up.

"Two people who weigh about the same." Marty got up too. "Abby, you and I can probably go at the same time."

"But what about . . ." Abby's voice trailed off as she looked at Theo and Sam.

Sam looked up at Theo. Theo looked down at Sam.

"There's no way." Sam shook his head. "We need two of me. At least."

"No," said Theo, sounding sort of cheerful—for Theo. "We need you and a really big rock."

While Sam and Theo hunted for a rock the right size, Abby and Marty got ready to cross. Marty looked tense, standing on the edge, and Abby, several yards away by the other plank, gave her a quick, nervous smile before, at exactly the same time, they both stepped out onto the bridge.

Each balanced on her plank, and Sam held his breath. For a moment he thought the bridge was wobbling, but it was an illusion—the planks were steady. The girls' weight had the scale balanced perfectly. Slowly, keeping pace with each other, they walked across.

"It's working!" Sam said.

"Great." Theo bent down and picked up a rock the size of a beach ball. "Here." He dumped it in Sam's arms.

Sam staggered. "Are you kidding? I have to walk across holding this thing?"

"No, you have to put that in your backpack. You walk across holding *this*." Theo held up another rock. Sam groaned.

"Are you sure this makes me as heavy as you?"

"How am I supposed to be sure? It's not like we have a scale handy."

"Well, there has to be some way that we can test it— never mind! Let's go now!" Sam said.

"What? Why?"

"Because that mountain lion must be *really* hungry."

Theo snapped his head around toward the tunnel entrance and saw what Sam had seen—the slinking shadow that had crept behind a stalagmite. "Don't run!" Theo said, bending down to pick up a handful of small rocks.

They backed slowly toward the bridge, Theo moving toward the left plank, Sam toward the right. "Come on!" Abby called urgently from the other side.

"We have to do it together," Sam said. "On three. One, two . . ."

The mountain lion seemed to sense that its prey was trying to escape. Its hindquarters bunched. It was preparing to leap.

Theo flung his handful of stones, and the cat, confused, jumped not at the boys, but at the incoming missiles.

"Three!" Sam yelled, and he and Theo stepped onto the planks, out over empty air.

The bridge wobbled. The mountain lion landed awkwardly, shifting its weight away from its injured front paw. It seemed confused by the bridge but unwilling to let its prey simply walk away. Keeping an eye on the boys, it crept closer to the edge of the ravine.

"Walk, walk, walk," Sam muttered. Hugging his rock to his middle, he took step by careful step, as Theo matched him on the other plank. Far below, Sam could hear the deep, hollow sound of water rushing past. They were hundreds of feet in the air, with only a few inches of wood between them and a drop into water that, from this height, would feel as hard as rock when they hit.

The plank was wide enough, the width of a sidewalk—there was no real reason Sam should fall. But all that empty space seemed to pull at him. He felt wobbly, and the burden of the rock in his arms and his backpack made it worse. Had they calculated the weight correctly? Did his rocks make him as heavy as Theo?

No, Sam realized. The rocks made him heavier. Not much, but some. The bridge was slowly starting to tip to the right.

"Watch out!" Marty called. "Sam, get rid of some weight!"

With an effort, Sam pitched the heavy rock he was holding over the side. It took a few hundred years to hear the splash.

It worked. The bridge slowly eased back into balance. Sam let out a huge sigh of relief, and they kept moving forward.

"Keep going!" Marty yelled. "Oh no!" Abby had gripped her arm tightly.

"Oh no *what*?" Sam shouted.

"Just—don't look back!"

Was there anybody in the world who, when told not to look back, didn't look back? "Theo, stop!" called Sam. They paused in the middle of the bridge, and Sam turned his head.

The mountain lion was still on the edge of the ravine behind them. It didn't seem to like the look of the planks, but it liked even less the idea that Sam and Theo were about to get away. It put out a huge paw and reached across the gap to touch the plank tentatively.

"Get moving!" Marty called sharply. "Now!"

The lion did not have to eat them to kill them, Sam realized, frozen with horror. All it had to do was decide to jump onto the bridge. Its weight would tip the mechanism, and all three of them—Sam, Theo, and the big cat—would plunge into the ravine.

"Sam, faster!" Theo ordered. Sam had to wrench his neck around to face forward. He hated not knowing what the mountain lion was doing behind him, but he had to look where he was going. If he didn't, he'd fall off the crazy bridge all by himself.

One step more, another, another. They didn't dare run. The other side of the ravine was ten yards away, then eight. It might as well have been a mile.

"What's that stupid cat doing?" Sam shouted to Marty.

"It's walking back and forth a little," she answered. "No—now it's kind of crouching. It's—"

"It's going to jump!" Abby shouted. "Run! Now!"

Sam and Theo ran. The bridge lurched. The mountain lion hissed. The edge of the ravine was getting closer—five yards, three, two, one!

"Jump!" Marty yelled. They jumped. Sam's feet flew over empty space, and then hit rock. He fell to his hands and knees, glancing sideways to make sure that Theo had made it too—just as the lion behind them leaped.

It hit the plank and yowled in distress, skidding to a stop and gripping the wood with its claws. The bridge was tipping. The cat didn't like that at all. It backed up clumsily as the bridge tipped more, and Sam felt himself holding his breath. The animal would have killed them, but he couldn't help it—he didn't want to see it tipped over the edge to its death.

"Maybe it can jump," Marty whispered.

"Jump, you stupid cat!" Sam yelled. "Get off!"

As if the mountain lion understood him, it twisted itself around on the plank to face the other side of the ravine. Only its claws kept it from falling as the bridge tipped further. The cat shrieked and then it seemed to fall and jump all at once. Its front paws reached the cave floor, while its back ones scrabbled at the ravine's wall. Then, with a slithering scramble, it got itself back on firm ground once more.

Marty let out her breath with a whoosh.

The cat seemed to have decided that this human prey was much more trouble than they were worth. It limped back toward the tunnel entrance without a backward glance.

"I'm glad," Marty said softly, watching it go.

"That thing wanted to eat us, Marty," Sam reminded her.

"I know. But still . . . Anyway, you were yelling for it to jump, Sam!"

"It was just being a wild animal," Abby said. "Acting on instinct. Predators have to hunt. It's not their fault."

"She's right," Theo said. "Animals don't have the capacity for evil. Only people have that."

Abby glanced up at Theo, and Sam saw a strange look pass across her face.

"Well, I'm still glad it's not going to be hunting me anymore," Sam replied. He got up, brushing grit and gravel off his hands and knees. He dumped the enormous rock from his pack and heaved the pack up onto his shoulders. "Where now?"

"There." Marty pointed.

Behind her, the cave branched into half a dozen tunnels. But it was pretty obvious that there was only one

Thomas Jefferson had wanted them to take. It was lined with wooden torches that had been mounted to the walls with iron brackets.

"At least we won't have to burn any more of my sweat-shirts," Sam said. He found the matches in his pack and pulled the first torch down from the wall, setting it alight. As they walked slowly down the tunnel, he lit each torch that they came to, and the smoky yellow light preceded them as they went deeper and deeper underground.

"It looks like it widens out a little more down here," Sam called back after they had been walking perhaps fifteen minutes. "Or a lot more, actually. Another cave, I think."

He was right. A little more walking brought them out into another cavern. More torches lined the walls. Abby took a second lit torch, and she and Sam moved quickly, getting every torch burning. Then they turned for a careful look at what was in the middle of the cave.

"You said there are always puzzles," Abby said, staring.

"Puzzles and games," Sam answered, nodding.

In the middle of the cave was a giant chessboard, with a game laid out, ready to be played.

The squares, dark and light, had been carved into the cave floor. Pawns and rooks and knights and bishops, made of black basalt or pale limestone, had been placed on their squares as if two giants had been interrupted midgame and wandered off, leaving the pieces set for when they returned.

"White's about to lose," Sam said, surveying the board. "The king is vulnerable."

"Maybe whoever built this was thinking about a real king," Theo said slowly. "Like George the Third. If we can checkmate the king . . . like Washington's army did to King George . . ."

"Checkmate means that the king cannot escape," Marty said. "It's based on a Persian phrase."

"Right!" Sam nodded. This was going to be a lot less scary than balancing on unsteady planks above an underground river while being stalked by a hungry predator. This was chess. Sam knew all about chess. He and Adam used to play after school. It was one of the oldest games in the world, and one of the best.

"See the black queen—there?" Sam pointed. "One move and she can checkmate the white king. Game over."

"Okay, do it." Theo nodded. Sam dropped his pack on the ground and moved onto the chessboard.

It felt strange, stepping among pieces nearly as tall as he was. He had been a piece on the board ever since he'd entered that American Dream competition, Sam thought. Flintlock, Arnold, even Evangeline and her Founders, had been moving him around from day one. Was he a pawn in their game, easy to sacrifice? Or something more important—a knight with its twisty, unexpected jumps, or a powerful rook, plowing straight across the board?

What he'd rather be, of course, was the chess master himself, the one who moved the pieces, the one who won the game. Well, now he had a chance. Sam reached the black queen, a smooth, curvy column of polished stone as tall as his shoulder. She sat in a groove carved into the stone floor, he saw. Simple. He'd just have to push her into the right place to checkmate the white king.

Sam took hold of the chess piece and pushed. It didn't budge. He braced his feet against the stone floor and shoved. The mechanism that let the piece move must have gotten rusty and dirty over the years, because when the black queen at last began to slide toward the white king, it set up a grating, grinding squeal that felt like it was shredding Sam's eardrums.

"Come on, lady," he gasped under his breath, pushing the queen on to the next square. "You want to win this game, don't you?"

But maybe the queen didn't. It got harder and harder to move her; she seemed almost to be pushing back, and she shook against his hands. He could hear his friends shouting, but with all the noise, he couldn't make out the words. Probably telling him not to give up. Well, he wouldn't. Sam shoved with all his strength, thrusting the queen one more square. Then something closed around his upper arm, yanking him away.

Startled, Sam looked up into Theo's horrified face. "Jeez! What?" Sam asked, panting. "I was getting it . . ."

He stopped speaking, suddenly understanding. It was not that the queen had been shaking under his hands; the entire cavern was shaking. Grit and dust rained down from the ceiling. Sam jumped to one side as a chunk of rock the size of his fist came down to shatter at his feet.

"You couldn't hear us yelling at you to stop," Theo told him as Sam stared around, wide-eyed. "This isn't—"

A tremendous *crash* cut off his words. A stalactite near the tunnel where they had entered had been worked loose by the tremors, and it crashed down, pulling more rock and debris with it to scatter and bounce and roll across the floor of the cave. The entrance to the tunnel was blocked in seconds.

Sam felt as if some of those rocks had landed on him. They were trapped.

CHAPTER EIGHT

"Don't just stand there!" Marty shouted at Sam. "Hurry!"

"Hurry where?" Sam shouted back at her across the heads of giant pawns and looming bishops, everything vibrating as tremors shook the cave. The motion had not stopped when Theo yanked Sam away from the black queen. This cave was going to shake itself to pieces. "Did you miss the fact that our exit just got blocked?" Sam yelled at Marty. "There's nowhere to go!"

"Then you've got to solve the puzzle," Abby called, coming to stand by Marty's shoulder. She gave Sam a firm look, and her chin came up. "Right? Isn't that what you always do? We have to solve the puzzle, then we can move forward."

Right. Abby was right. Sam shook his head a little, trying to jar his thoughts into motion. That was how the Founders always worked. *Solve the puzzle, Sam*, he told himself. *That's why you're here.*

"Theo!" Sam said. "Shove the queen back where she was." Theo grabbed the queen and pushed, moving her much faster than Sam had been able to do. It wasn't just that Theo was stronger. She moved more easily in that direction, and the dreadful screeching noise she'd made was gone too.

But when she slid back onto her original square, the shaking did not stop. Gravel from the ceiling scattered down over Sam. He brushed it out of his eyes, frowning.

So moving the queen had been wrong—obviously. But getting her back where she'd been hadn't solved the problem. Fixing the wrong move hadn't been enough. They had to make the *right* move.

With a grating *crack*, a wall of the cavern fell into the cave, torches coming down with it, their flames choked by grit and debris. Rocks and pebbles spilled and bounced across the floor. Abby grabbed Marty's arm and pulled her out of the way of a giant chunk of rock that rolled to a stop right where she'd been standing.

They had to make the right move *now*.

The cave was falling apart around him, his friends were in danger, *he* was in danger—and Sam couldn't let himself

think about any of it. He turned back to the board that
surrounded him. Think about chess. Only about chess.

Look at the pieces, he told himself. *See how they connect.*
Chess was never just about how each piece moved; it was
about each piece's relationship with the others. Which
was vulnerable? Which was powerful? It all depended on
where it stood and who stood with it.

The white king was in danger from the black queen—
but that hadn't been the right move. There had to be
others—yes! That black bishop could checkmate the white
king too. Sam took a step forward and stopped.

See all the pieces. Look at the whole board. He'd jumped
in too quickly the first time and moved the black queen
without checking to see if that was the only move he
could make. That had been wrong. He couldn't afford to
be wrong twice.

"Marty!" he yelled. "Do you play chess?"

Marty shook her head. "Scrabble!" she shouted back.

"But you know the moves?" he called. She nodded.
"See the bishop? Anything else? Anything I missed?"

"Don't take too long," Theo said, his voice soft enough
to undercut the grinding of stone on stone that filled
the cave.

Sam nodded, but he didn't move. Black queen to
checkmate—wrong. Black bishop to checkmate—maybe.
And there, on the edge of the board . . .

Marty saw it at the same instant Sam did.

"Black pawn!" she shouted, and Sam nodded. Black pawn to checkmate the white king.

Which move was right? Bishop or pawn?

"'Every citizen should be a soldier,'" Marty called out. Sam looked over at her, startled. "Thomas Jefferson said that," she told him, her eyes meeting his over the oversized chess pieces. Over knights and bishops, kings and queens . . . and pawns.

Sam grinned. Who'd won the American Revolution? Who'd checkmated King George III? Not another king or queen, not a bishop or a knight—an army of ordinary citizens who'd decided they wanted to rule themselves.

The pawn was the right move!

Sam jumped to the pawn. There was a groove in place at its base, and Sam put his shoulder to the piece and shoved with all his might. The black pawn shot easily along the groove, leaving Sam staggering. It smacked into the white king, and the tall chess piece, topped with a spiky crown, wobbled on its base and crashed to the floor, shattering into fragments.

The next thing Sam knew, another wall collapsed with a crash like thunder.

Sam ducked to the ground instinctively as clouds of dust billowed up. He'd been wrong! How could it have happened? He'd been so sure the black pawn was the right move. It had made so much sense. And now . . . had he killed them all? Sam covered his head and waited for the ceiling of the cave to come down, burying them in a tomb. *Sorry, Marty. Sorry, Theo. Sorry, Abby. Sorry, sorry, sorry* . . .

He waited a few more seconds. No ceiling fell.

Cautiously, Sam lifted his head, fanning dust away from his face. Theo was sitting up next to him, and he could hear the girls coughing and spluttering to his right, although he couldn't see them yet. Shafts of bright sunlight shone through the clouds of dirt, and as the gray powder slowly settled, Sam realized that he hadn't doomed them, after all.

He'd made the right move.

The wall that had fallen apart revealed a bright summer day outside. When the black pawn had checkmated the white king, it had opened up the way out.

Abby and Marty, clinging to each other, made their way through the chessboard to Sam and Theo's side. Coated from head to toe in dust, they looked like ghosts. Sam glanced down at himself. He looked the same.

"Sam." Abby let go of Marty, rubbed her eyes, and smiled at him. "That was—wow. You're amazing. You got to that pawn just in time. You saved us all!" Her smile grew wider; her eyes glowed with admiration. Sam felt pleasure bubbling up to replace his ebbing terror. Now that he thought about it, choosing the black pawn *had* been a

pretty slick move. And it was nice to get a little apprecia-
tion, for sure.

Marty coughed, wiping dust and grit from her glasses.
"Sure, all by himself," she said with a sour look at both
Abby and Sam. "Anyway, we'd better get out. This cave
might not be too stable."

"Wait." Theo crawled over to the shattered remains
of the white king and pushed some of the broken pieces
aside. "There's something here . . ." He picked up a stone
urn about six inches high.

"Let's look at it outside, okay?" Sam got up, and the
four of them climbed over tumbled boulders and broken
slabs of rock to reach the fresh air.

Blinking in the light, Sam sat down on soft grass with
a sigh. He used both hands to rub stone dust out of his
hair. They were in a small meadow at the base of a tall cliff,
a meadow that formed one end of a long, narrow valley.
There was sunshine, there were flowers, there were even
butterflies. Butterflies! Sam could hardly believe it. He felt
as if he'd walked out of a horror movie and right into a
commercial for fabric softener.

The valley stretched for miles, with mountains on
either side. It looked to Sam like there were only two ways
to get to this meadow—by taking a very long and treach-
erous hike up that valley, or climbing through the cave
system they'd just left.

He flopped back on the grass, staring up at the blue sky. Well, mostly blue. Maybe half blue. Dark clouds were starting to pile up off to his left. But for the moment, the sun was warm on his face, birds were twittering away in the trees, and Marty and Theo were busy talking. Sam turned his head to one side to see what they were so worried about. They were bent over the urn that Theo had picked up from the broken pieces of the white king. Abby was looking over their shoulders.

"The Founders' symbol," Theo was saying, pointing to something on the urn. "See? This must be the next clue."

"And it says 'Josiah Hodge,'" Abby said, leaning in. "My ancestor! Do you think he left this inside that chess piece?"

"There are some other words too," Marty said. "Sam! Come and look at this."

Sam groaned. Nobody got to rest for two seconds, not while Marty was around. He heaved himself up off the nice comfortable ground and came over to look at the urn. Theo rubbed away dust that had settled on the smooth stone, and all of them read the inscription carved under the Founders' symbol—a pyramid with the eye above and Jefferson's quill inside.

The tree of liberty must be refreshed from time to time
with the blood of patriots and tyrants.

Sam glanced up at Marty. "Thomas Jefferson again, I presume?" She nodded. "Kind of a creepy thing to say."

"He meant that we can't take freedom for granted," Marty said, giving Sam a stern look.

"I guess. But this urn is kind of creepy looking too," Sam pointed out. He could feel his puzzle-solving brain stirring into life. This urn was their next clue—but what was it telling them? To look for a tree? They were surrounded by millions of trees. There must be some other clue somewhere. "It looks kind of like the thing we got from the funeral parlor when my great-aunt Susan died," he went on. "For her ashes."

"Sam, that's just . . . ew." Marty grimaced as Theo put one of his huge hands around the top of the urn and gave it a twist. The top came off.

"Gross but accurate," Theo said, peering into the urn. "He's right."

"Ugh." Sam leaned over to glance at the pile of pale dust that sat inside the urn. "Meet Josiah, everybody. Abby, I think that's your ancestor in there."

Abby made a face. "Oh my—that's—Theo, close it!" Theo did so, twisting the lid to seal it. The lid was strangely shaped, Sam noticed—all around its top edge was a jagged pattern of triangles, like a mountain range.

It looked something like a key, if there were a lock somewhere that a circular key could fit into.

"So we have ashes and a weird urn and a quote about blood and trees," Sam said with a sigh. He brushed the rest of the dirt off his clothes and looked around. "Where do we go from here?"

"We also have a storm blowing in," Abby said, looking up at the sky as the sunlight vanished. The clouds Sam had noticed earlier had closed in even farther, blocking the light.

"Remember the weather forecast back in Whitefish?" Marty asked.

Sam groaned. He did remember. Storms, lightning, flash floods.

"We'd better get under cover first," Abby said. "And figure out what to do with that urn second."

Their initial thought was to shelter in the cave, but as they looked back in, an ominous rumble and a shower of rocks from the ceiling convinced them that wasn't the best idea. Theo stowed Josiah's urn in Sam's backpack, and they quickly made their way down the valley as the sky darkened overhead and the air grew cooler by the minute. Soon they were under the cover of thick trees, walking over knobby roots and deep drifts of pine needles, scrambling up and across stony ledges. At last they stumbled onto a flat stretch of ground where the going was easier.

"We could build a lean-to, maybe," Abby said as she walked beside Sam, with Theo and Marty behind them. "Or find another cave."

"You really think a lean-to is going to keep us dry?" Sam asked, peering up at the bits of cloudy sky he could see through the thick branches overhead.

"Better than nothing," Abby pointed out. "Or . . . wait." She looked around and started to smile.

"What?"

"Or we could just keep going, because I think this is a road."

"A road?" Sam looked down at his feet, tromping over mud and scraggly grass. "Doesn't look like one to me. And who'd build a road out here?"

Abby's smile grew wider. "Loggers, maybe. Or hunters. I know it doesn't look like much, but see how straight it is?" She pointed ahead, where Sam could indeed see a narrow stretch of roughly flat ground, free of large trees. "Nothing in the wilderness goes in a straight line, not for long. If we follow this, it might lead us somewhere before the storm hits. It's worth a try."

Sam nodded, and the four of them pressed on. Sam wasn't quite convinced that Abby was right about the thing they were following being a road. It was rocky and overgrown, with brush crowding in from the side and the occasional sapling right in the middle.

But then Abby kicked aside some fallen leaves to point out marks that had been scraped onto a flat stretch of stone. "Wheel marks, I bet." Sam peered at the crisscrossing tracks, faint and narrow. He'd never have noticed if Abby hadn't pointed them out. "Not tires—wooden wheels. From wagons, probably."

"So this really was a road," Marty said, nodding. "A long time ago, at least."

"Better keep going," Theo said. And they did, until suddenly Abby whooped in triumph.

"Yes! Up ahead! Buildings!"

"What kind of buildings?" Sam peered through the trees. "A ranger station? A Starbucks?"

Behind Sam, Marty sighed. Now Sam could see what Abby meant—through the green, he glimpsed wooden walls and bits of mossy roof. They hurried on, and at last broke free of the trees and into . . .

A town?

Sam shook his head in wonder. He'd been hoping for a hunter's cabin maybe, and what he got was a dozen buildings clustered together. They'd been built of logs, all except one no more than a single story high. Here and there half a chimney remained, poking up above a tumbledown wall. Trees had grown up under broken roofs; vines were doing their best to pull down entire structures.

The tallest building seemed to be in the best condition. It had a peaked roof that was still mostly intact. A cross, made of two logs nailed together, loomed over the door, which was still propped in its frame.

"A church," Marty said, shaking her head in amazement. "This was a town once! People lived here. I wonder if the park even knows about it?"

"I've never seen it on a map," Abby said. "But not every old farm or settlement makes it onto the maps."

"Score one for Abby!" Sam gave her a high five, and she looked pleased. "Good call on following that old road."

"How old *was* that road?" Marty asked suddenly, her eyes narrowing as if a fresh idea had hit her.

"I don't know." Abby shrugged. "Those wheel ruts weren't made yesterday. A hundred years old, maybe? More?"

"So it could have been a new road when that chess game was made? When Josiah's ashes were hidden in the white king?"

"I guess," Abby answered, looking a little puzzled. But Sam wasn't.

"You think maybe we were supposed to follow that road?" he asked Marty. "We were supposed to end up here?"

"To end up here with Josiah's ashes." Marty looked around with purpose in her gaze. "You noticed how the top of that urn looks kind of like a key, Sam?"

"Sure."

"Maybe what it unlocks is here."

An hour later, they gathered together again in front of the ancient church. "Anything?" Sam asked hopefully. Then he looked at the faces of Marty, Abby, and Theo, and felt the hope drain from his own.

Nobody had found a lock that a circular key could open. Nobody, it turned out, had found a lock at all.

They'd split up to look all around the ghost town, and while Sam had found a lot of dirt, moss, mushrooms, and rotten logs, he'd found nothing else. When people had walked away from this town, they had not been planning on coming back. Nothing had been left behind but what they couldn't move—the walls, roofs, doors, and empty windows of their abandoned houses.

Everybody else, it seemed, had found the same thing. "I was so sure," Marty said mournfully, shaking her head, as she looked up and down the single street. "The next clue—I really thought it would be here."

A cold, fat raindrop plopped down on Sam's head, and on the horizon, there was a quick flash of light and a long, rumbling boom.

"Better get under cover," Theo said, nodding at the church. "We can hunt more in the morning."

They headed up the two stone stairs that led to the church's door, which hung cockeyed from a single hinge. When Theo tried to lift the door and push it open, it simply fell over with a thud onto the floor inside.

Following Marty in, Sam paused, noticing some deep scratches on the wooden doorframe above his head. He reached up but could not touch the splintery spots where wood had been gouged from the frame. "What did that?" he wondered out loud.

"Bear," Abby said from behind him. She'd pulled up her hood, and raindrops were splashing on it.

"Bear?" Sam repeated in disbelief.

She nodded, as if it were the most obvious thing in the world. "Grizzly, to be up that high," she told Sam. "They leave marks like that on trees too. Anything they can scratch or bite. Just kind of letting the world know they've been here. Come on, Sam; it's getting wet out here." She pushed past him into the church.

Bears. It wasn't enough that he had to face killer chess games and other delightful Founder pastimes; he also had to think about flash floods, mountain lions, and bears. Sam groaned to himself and shook his head as he followed her.

The church wasn't much bigger than Sam's homeroom class. No pews or furniture were left, but the door must have kept out most of the animal life and maybe a bit of the weather, since the walls were still standing and only one corner of the roof had fallen in. They settled down as far away as they could get from the rain pelting in through the hole, huddled in the opposite corner on the damp, dirty floor. Marty pulled out her flashlight, which cast a circle of warm yellow light into the gloom.

"Here," she said, digging back into the pack. "Rain ponchos. We can spread them out and sit on them. Protein bars. Some trail mix. Water."

"Where are the s'mores?" Sam asked. Marty frowned at him, and Abby flashed him a quick smile, her teeth bright in the gloom. "Hot dogs?" Sam suggested. "Anybody know all the words to 'Kumbaya'?"

"What are you offering toward our survival, Sam?" Marty asked.

Sam pulled open his own pack to see what he had. "First, we can't leave out our friend Josiah." He set Josiah's ashes up alongside the wall and gave the urn a pat. "And . . . let's see." He dug into his pack. "Snickers. Kit Kats. And Oreos. Who wants what?" He touched something heavy and square at the bottom of his pack and pulled it out. It was Arnold's satellite phone.

He sat looking at it for a moment, with a shiver that wasn't caused by the wind swirling through the broken roof and empty windows of the church. He had not exactly forgotten Gideon Arnold—once he'd met the guy, that wasn't possible. But crossing dangerous bridges and getting stalked by mountain lions and playing deadly chess games in underground caverns did tend to concentrate his mind on what was at hand—solving the puzzles. Surviving.

And once they'd solved all the puzzles . . . if they ever did . . . if they got out of this wilderness and found what they were looking for, what then? Sam remembered, with a sinking feeling, that he'd never come up with an answer to that question. Would they really just pick up the phone and give Gideon Arnold a call?

Sam was tempted to stuff the phone back inside his pack. But it was too late—the others had seen it too. He set it down on the grimy wooden floor, rubbing his hands on his jeans as if the phone had contaminated him.

"Should we . . ." Abby hesitated. "Call him? That Arnold guy?"

"Why?" Theo asked.

"Just to . . . I guess . . . tell him we're working on it. That we've found the cave and got Josiah's ashes. So he knows we're getting closer to finding it. To getting the Quill."

"If we find the Quill—when we find the Quill—we've got to keep it safe," Theo answered. He was hunched over against the cold, his hood pulled up over his head. His voice seemed to be coming out of a puddle of shadow. "We're not handing it over to Gideon Arnold."

"What are you talking about?" Abby's shocked face went pale in the flashlight's beam; her light hair looked close to white against the dark walls of the old church. "We've *got* to hand it over! You heard that guy. He's going to kill my parents unless we give him the Quill!"

"He's going to kill your parents anyway," Theo said. His voice was flat and cold and heavy. "And Evangeline. He probably already has."

The shock of Theo's words hit Sam as hard as if the big guy had suddenly turned and punched him in the stomach. Marty sat up straight, drawing in a quick breath. Abby turned even paler and looked as if she were about to throw up.

It seemed to take Sam a long time to suck in enough air to speak. "Theo," he choked out finally. "Harsh, man. You don't know that."

Theo's head turned toward Sam quickly. "You've met Arnold, Sam. You know perfectly well what he's capable of. What are we supposed to do, pretend? It doesn't do us any good. Gideon Arnold is not going to let any prisoner go."

Sam was shaking his head. "We can't just give up on them, Theo! This is Abby's mom and dad we're talking about."

"Would you say that if it was *your* parents he'd kidnapped?" Abby demanded, right on the heels of Sam's words. "Would it be so easy to just let them . . ." She choked. "To let them . . ."

"He probably did kidnap my mother," Theo answered, any emotion he was feeling carefully controlled. "If he didn't just kill her. She knew the risks. So did Evangeline. They promised to protect the Founders' secret with their lives. I did too. That doesn't include handing any one of the Founders' artifacts over to Gideon Arnold."

"But, Theo, man—"

"No, Sam." Marty leaned forward into the light, her face somber. "He's right."

"Marty, you too? You're kidding me!"

"Sam, this is bigger than any one person. I'm sorry, Abby. Truly I am." Marty reached out a hand to Abby, who shrank back, her face taut with misery. "We can't let a man like Gideon Arnold anywhere near Benjamin Franklin's secret weapon. No matter who gets hurt."

Sam could hardly believe his ears. He'd kind of expected this out of Theo's mouth—but Marty?

Two days ago, one of Gideon Arnold's thugs had been about to strangle Marty, and Sam had given Arnold the information he'd asked for to save her life. It hadn't even occurred to him to do anything else. If he'd been the one choking for air and Marty had the information in her hand, would she have done the same for him?

What if it were Sam, rather than Evangeline and the Hodges, in Gideon Arnold's clutches right now?

"I can't believe you, Marty." Sam looked at Abby's stricken face and felt anger, sharp and hot, flare up inside his chest. "You sound just like a Founder. Anything's okay as long as it protects the secret, huh?" He turned to Theo and shook his head. "It's okay to lie, to risk people's lives, to abandon our friends?"

Theo stood up suddenly and shook off his hood. He glared down at Sam, and spat a single word at him.

"*Yes.*"

Theo lifted up his foot in its heavy hiking boot and put it down squarely on Gideon Arnold's phone, crushing it and grinding the black splinters into the wooden floor.

CHAPTER NINE

On the whole, it was one of the worst nights of Sam's life.

Outside, thunder pounded the sky and rain hammered at the boards of the old church. Inside, the storm had been just as bad. Abby screamed at Theo, Marty tried to calm her down, Theo sat in a corner and refused to talk to anyone, and Sam didn't know what to say or even how to feel.

At last Abby, furious and tearful, picked up a rain poncho and her jacket and went over to lie down in a corner as far away from all of them as she could get. After a while, Sam had gone to sit next to her, leaving Theo and Marty on their own.

Sam sat there wrapped in his fleece jacket, his cold hands in his pockets, and shivered while ideas chased themselves through his mind, each more miserable than the last.

Sam understood Theo and Marty—he did. Sam had promised to help safeguard Benjamin Franklin's weapon, and he knew firsthand how scary Gideon Arnold truly was. But he understood Abby too. It was her parents they were talking about. If it had been Sam's mother and father in Gideon Arnold's clutches . . . Sam knew he'd have given over the Quill in two seconds to keep them safe. Maybe it wouldn't have been the smartest thing to do, but he'd do it, and without a second thought.

So who was right—Theo or Abby? Both. Neither. Sam had no idea. He was cold and tired, and it seemed completely impossible to fall asleep, but eventually he must have done so, because suddenly he found himself waking up, blinking in a weird, lifeless gray light. The storm had blown itself out. Even though the air was still damp and chilly, everything was quiet—no whisper of wind, no rattling of rain, no crack of thunder.

Abby was asleep next to him, the blotches of tears still on her cheeks. Sam didn't want to wake her up. There was nothing he could say that would make her feel better, and plenty of ways to make her feel worse. Theo and Marty were asleep on the other side of the church. He didn't much feel like talking to them either.

Sam got up, grabbed his hiking boots from where he'd left them the night before, and slipped out of the church. The ghost town looked, well, ghostly, in the grayish light that comes before the sun slides up over the horizon. Restlessly, Sam headed down the two stone steps and into the street, walking past tumbledown cabins with empty doorways and blank spaces where windows had once been. As soon as he got to the end of the town, he turned and came back.

What were they supposed to do now that Theo had smashed the phone? They had no way of contacting Gideon Arnold, and no way of handing Jefferson's Quill over to him. To Theo, of course, that was a good thing. Theodore Washington wasn't going to play Gideon Arnold's game—and he wasn't about to let the rest of them play either.

Sam sighed and rubbed his hands over his face, trying to grind the sleep out of his eyes and the stiffness out of his brain. They still had to find the Quill, didn't they? What other choice did they have? It wasn't like Sam could just hike out of here and catch a plane home. Not knowing what he knew about Gideon Arnold and the damage the man could do—to Evangeline, to Abby's parents, to the country, to the world.

It looked like there was only one thing to do—find the Quill and keep it safe. Just like Theo had wanted all along. The big guy had wiped all the other moves off the board.

But it didn't mean Sam had to like it. And he didn't blame Abby for not liking it either.

He was back at the church steps now, but he didn't feel like going in. Sam wandered around the building, kicking his way through wet, knee-high grass, and stubbed his toe so hard on a rock he nearly yelped with pain. Hopping away, he tripped over another rock and fell.

Then he realized that what he had fallen over wasn't a rock—it was a tombstone.

Great. He was in the church's graveyard. If that wasn't the perfect setting for his mood this morning . . .

Sam got up and walked among the tombs, brushing aside clinging grass to read old names and dates. One of the tombstones seemed larger than the rest, with a lot of writing on it. Sam made his way over to that one and crouched down to read what it said.

It was odd. He wiped dew away from the stone and then rubbed harder, cleaning off moss and lichen. Some of the letters were missing, and it didn't look as if they'd worn away naturally with time either. It looked like they'd never been carved.

FRE—MAN JOSS—OFT
BELO—ED SON, H—SBAND, F—IEND
AN A—ERIC—N PATRI—T

BO—N 1743 D—ED 1826

RE—EM—ER ME AS YOU —ASS BY,
AS Y—U ARE —OW, SO ON—E WAS I,
—S I AM N—W, —O YOU M—ST BE,
—REPARE FO— —EATH AND —OL—OW M—.

Who would carve a tombstone and leave out half the letters?

Maybe someone with a message to send.

Sam's heart speeded up, and he felt a familiar excitement fizzing along his nerves. It didn't exactly burn away the resentment he felt toward Theo, who'd taken it upon himself to decide what their next move should be, or Marty, who'd sided with Theo—but it did shove those dark feelings into the back of Sam's mind for the moment. Because this was it! He'd found it! Their next clue!

In ten minutes he had everybody awake and outside to check it out. Neither Theo nor Abby was saying much, and in fact, nobody seemed happy with anybody else. But they were all willing to follow Sam outside, focus on the tombstone, and leave last night's bitter argument alone— for now.

"Right." Marty, in particular, seemed extremely relieved to have a puzzle to think about. "The first thing is the missing letters—obviously." She dug into her pack and pulled out a notebook and a pen.

"Obviously," Sam agreed. Abby moved to Sam's side, farther away from Theo, and studied the tombstone too. "But that first line—I don't get what's missing there."

"It's a name," Marty said, sucking on her pen.

"No kidding. But we don't know what name. It's not like it's a simple one."

"Like Sam," Marty agreed. She quickly copied down the epitaph in her notebook. "Skip that for now. What about the rest of the lines?"

That was easier. It didn't take long before they had the message mostly deciphered.

FRE__MAN JOSS__OFT
BELOVED SON, HUSBAND, FRIEND
AN AMERICAN PATRIOT

BORN 1743 DIED 1826

REMEMBER ME AS YOU PASS BY,
AS YOU ARE NOW, SO ONCE WAS I,
AS I AM NOW, SO YOU MUST BE,
PREPARE FOR DEATH AND FOLLOW ME.

"Whoa," Sam muttered. "Morbid much?"

"Okay," Marty muttered, scribbling fast. "So if we pull out all the letters we just filled in, minus those first two we don't know yet, we get . . . this."

__ __V U R M A O R I M B P O N C A O S U P
R D F L E

"A code," Sam said.

"A code," Marty agreed.

Theo spoke up. "Can you break it?"

Sam snorted. "With one hand tied behind my back. With one eye shut. With—"

Marty shoved the notebook at him. "With a little less showing off?"

Sam felt the tight clench inside his stomach relaxing. They had a puzzle to solve, and he and Marty were working on it together. Things weren't quite right among the four of them, but at least they could still do this.

"Maybe you just have to rearrange the letters," Sam muttered to himself, scribbling possibilities. "There's *PRE*, that's a common prefix . . . or *ED*, could be an ending. There's *AIM*, that's a word!"

"But there are hardly any *E*s," Marty said, looking at what Sam was doing. "And *E* is the most common letter in English."

"I know that, Marty. Who doesn't know that?"

"And a lot of *U*s. I always hate getting a *U* in Scrabble; it's really hard to work with. Sam, I don't think this is right way to go."

"Maybe not." Sam's letter combinations weren't getting him much of anywhere, he had to admit. "It's not a simple offset code either. You know, using *B* for *A* and *C* for *B*, and so on."

"I got that already," Marty told him a little smugly.

"It would help if the letters were broken up into words."

"But they're not. What's the most common letter in the message?"

"Uh . . . R. Three Rs."

"So maybe R is E?"

Sam scribbled Es over the Rs in the message but shook his head. "It doesn't help us much."

"We've just got to keep trying." Marty took the pen and notebook back. "T is the next most common letter in English, after E. What's the second most frequent letter in the code?"

Sam stared at the message, counting. "It's no good. Two As, two Ms, three Os, two Us. Any of those letters could be T. This isn't working. We can't just try letters randomly."

"So you're giving up?"

"Let me think." Sam's fingers tapped impatiently on a tombstone. "It's a code. A secret message. It isn't any good sending somebody a secret message unless they have the key to breaking it. So either the key is something easy to figure out—in which case why aren't we figuring it out? Or it's something . . ."

A wide grin spread across Marty's face. "Or it's something we already have."

Sam's grin was just as wide. "You do have it, right?"

Abby spoke up for the first time. "Have what?"

"Have what Thomas Jefferson meant us to have." Marty turned to her pack, beside her on the grass. "Here!" She pulled out the wheel cipher that they had found hidden in the wall of Caractacus Ranch.

"Try it," Sam said eagerly.

"We still don't know the first two letters. I'll start with the third wheel in." Marty deftly spun the small wooden wheels on their long spoke, making a row of letters that matched what she'd written in her notebook. "Now, if this works—"

"It'll work," Sam said. His fingers were tingling; he felt the hair on the back of his neck prickle.

"Overconfidence is a killer," Marty told him, but he could tell from her voice that her heart wasn't in the scolding. "*If* this works, one of the rows of letters on the cipher should hold a message we can read." She rotated the cipher wheel slowly. Sam ached to snatch it from her, but if he did that he'd just jostle the letters and they'd have to start all over. Meaningless rows of letters passed before his eyes:

```
U X E D L G Z C K M T D T H L I Y F H J Z P G Y Z J
Y A V U R M A O R I M B P O N C A O S U P R D F L E
P I I T E D W E S T A N D D I V I D E D W E F A L L
L N O S X A V H V I R Z B K D K T W U W V T V X N B
```

"That's it!" he yelled. Abby jumped.

Theo frowned. "Keep your voice down, Sam."

"Why, because the bears are going to hear us? That's it, there!" He pointed. "See, Marty? Can you tell what the first two letters should be?"

"Of course I can!" Marty spun the first two wheels and turned up the letters *U* and *N.*

| M A E D L G Z C K M T D T H L I Y F H J Z C G Y Z J |
| E H V U R M A O R I M B P O N C A O S U P R D F L E |
| U N I T E D W E S T A N D D I V I D E D W E F A L L |
| Y O O S X A V H V I R Z B K D K T W U W V H V X N B |

"United we stand, divided we fall," Sam read out loud.

"And that means that the missing letters in the name on the tombstone are . . ." Marty turned the wheel back to check their original line of coded text. "*R* and *I.*"

"Does that really matter?" Sam asked.

Marty ignored him. "So the name on the tombstone is Freeman Josshoft. That's an odd name. Maybe it's Dutch . . ."

Sam laughed. "Dutch! Marty, you're better than that." Staring at all those little letters on the cipher wheel must have made letters dance inside his brain, because it was easy to see now why the name on the tombstone was so odd. "It's an anagram. Mix up the letters."

"Thomas Jefferson!" Marty gasped. "Rearrange the letters in 'Freeman Josshoft' and you get 'Thomas Jefferson'!"

"Just a little extra clue so we know we're on the right track," Sam told her happily. It felt right, solving a puzzle with Marty. She seemed to feel the same way.

Then Abby spoke up, and her cool voice cast a shadow over the triumph. "So we've got the clue. But what are we supposed to do with it? It's not exactly a direction."

"It's never that simple." Sam looked up from the tombstone and rubbed his eyes. "But it'll be somewhere around here. We know we're where old TJ—"

"Really, Sam, I don't think you should call him that."

Sam ignored Marty. "—wanted us to be. So something near here will . . . um . . . unite. I guess."

Marty had her map out and was spreading it out on the wet grass. "Unite. Unite," she said, chewing on a strand of her black hair. "Two things coming together . . ."

Sam turned in a slow circle. Marty had the right idea. Two things coming together . . .

"There!" they both said at the same moment.

Sam looked down at Marty, and she looked up at him.

"What's there?" she asked.

"What did you find?" he asked.

She pointed to her map. "Look here, at all those streams. Down at the end of the valley, they all run into this river. Uniting, right? Many becoming one? Just like all the colonies had to unite together to win the Revolution?"

"Or over there," Sam said. "Look down the street, to the end of the valley." The just-risen sun illuminated two cliffs that rose up above the tree line, meeting at a sharp angle that looked very much like a pyramid to Sam. "Two cliffs uniting into one. And doesn't that look kind of Founderish to you? They did love their pyramids."

"There can't be two right answers," Abby said, still sounding a little cold.

"I vote for the river," Sam said. "Lots of streams, all coming together—that's a better fit than two cliffs. It took a lot of colonies coming together to win the Revolution."

"No, the cliffs," Marty said just as quickly. "The Founders would have seen that pyramid and used it, for sure."

"Marty, come on. It's got to be the river."

"Sam, that river might have changed course twenty times since the Civil War. But those cliffs have probably been like that since the Cretaceous!"

"Arguing isn't going to solve this one," Theo said, not sounding much more cheerful than Abby. "Two possibilities. We'd better check them both out."

"I'll go with Sam," Abby said quickly. "To the river."

Marty stood, folding up her map. "Then Theo and I can head over to those cliffs, I guess. Meet back here in three hours?"

She looked over at Sam, and he thought he saw something anxious in her eyes. Splitting up? It did make good sense . . . but Sam had a moment of hesitation.

He'd only met Theo and Marty a few days ago. But it had been an *intense* few days. And everything the three of them had done, they'd done together.

But they did need to investigate both the river and the cliffs. So he grinned reassuringly at Marty and saluted.

"Three hours, Captain! Should we synchronize our watches?"

Marty rolled her eyes. "Just don't fall in the river and drown, Sam."

Sam and Abby left Theo waiting while Marty repacked and organized her backpack. Following Marty's map, they located one of the streams and set out to follow it to the larger river.

"Listen, Abby," Sam said, after they had hiked in silence for a while. "I want you to know—I'm not giving up on your parents. No matter what Theo says."

"Thanks, Sam." Abby sniffed hard. She was in front of Sam; he couldn't see her face. But he could hear the gratitude in her voice. A few minutes later she asked, "How long have you known them? Marty and Theo?"

"Actually, just a few days. Remember, I told you how we met on the way to Death Valley?"

Abby nodded. There was a pause, during which the loudest sound was the crunch of their boots over dead leaves. Then Abby said, "Sam . . . I think you should be careful."

"Me? Why?" Of course they should all be careful; they had Gideon Arnold on their tail and killer puzzles from the Founders of the country to solve. But why should Sam be more careful than anyone else?

"You're not like them," Abby told him.

"Huh?"

"Would you have smashed that phone last night?"

"Well . . . no." Sam had to admit it. Maybe he wouldn't cheerfully hand Thomas Jefferson's Quill over to the bad guys, but Sam wouldn't have smashed the phone, not unless he had no other choice. If you wanted to win a game, there was no point in cutting off options until you had to. It was better to keep as many moves as possible in play.

"That Theo . . . he's kind of brainwashed Marty, hasn't he?" Abby kept walking, moving in and out of shadow as she walked beneath trees and back out into the sunlight. Sam couldn't see her face, but he could hear her clearly as her voice drifted back to him.

"Brainwashed? Listen, Abby, I know you're mad at Theo. I don't blame you. I'm not thrilled with him either. But brainwashing—that's way too extreme. Theo's just serious. About the Founders. About everything."

"And he's starting to get Marty thinking the way he does," Abby said. "That whatever the Founders want is more important than anything else. Than my parents. Than the rest of the world." On a flat piece of rock by the edge of the stream, she stopped, turning to face Sam. A breeze blew tendrils of her light hair around her thin face, and her clear blue eyes were solemn. "I mean it, Sam. I think you should watch out for yourself. Theo's made it pretty clear he doesn't care what happens to anyone else, as long as he gets what he wants."

Sam was shaking his head. "No, Abby, really. You've got the wrong idea."

Abby shrugged. "I don't expect you to agree with me, Sam. Not right now. But don't forget what I said, okay? Let's keep going."

They kept going, Sam with a squirmy, uneasy feeling inside. Abby was upset, and who could blame her? But it was crazy to talk about brainwashing. To suggest that Sam needed to watch out for Theo. How many times since this whole thing had started had Theo saved Sam's life?

Of course, Sam's life would not have been in any danger at all if it hadn't been for Theo, and for Evangeline too. If those two hadn't lied to him, told him he'd won a contest, and dragged him along on a life-and-death mission because they needed somebody good at solving puzzles.

Sam pulled a Snickers bar out of his pack and ate it as he walked, but not even the melty goodness of chocolate and caramel could wash away the bad taste in his mouth.

The stream headed downhill, getting deeper and faster as they followed it. Sam stuffed his half-eaten chocolate bar into the outside pocket of his backpack as they walked out from beneath the shadows of the trees. Here the stream spilled into a wide but shallow river that meandered across a rocky plain. It wasn't the only stream to do so either.

"United we stand," Sam said, looking around. "So . . . anything like a clue here?"

Abby pointed. "Like that?"

Sam spun around and blinked, dazzled. A bright light had flashed right in his eyes. Sam rubbed them until the black-and-blue spots had faded from his vision, and he saw that the light was coming from somewhere back the way they had come, flashing through the branches of the trees.

"What is that?" Abby asked. "It could be just the light reflecting off water somewhere, I guess, but—"

"Not unless there's a river around here that knows Morse code," Sam answered.

The light was flashing rhythmically, long and short. In his head, Sam translated the blinks:

—••• • •— •—• —• •

Morse code was just another code, after all. And it was a handy thing to know if you liked solving puzzles.

Sam had memorized it last summer. This was a short message and pretty easy to figure out: BEAR NE.

"Bear northeast," he muttered. "It's Marty, of course. She must have a mirror in her pack"—of course Marty would have a mirror, Sam thought to himself—"and she's flashing us a message. I bet they can see the next clue from wherever they are. Up on that cliff, I guess." So Marty had been right about the cliff, and he'd been wrong about the river. Sam stifled a groan.

"And she wants us to go northeast?" Abby asked.

"Looks like it." Sam turned around until he was facing the direction the sun had risen. "That's east, so . . ." He and Abby figured out northeast and headed that way, along the bank of the river, forcing their way through alder thickets and clambering over stones.

The flashing light continued blinking away through the trees. Sam lifted his hand to shield his eyes. "We got it, Marty!" He took off his hat and waved it, trying to signal. "If she can see us to flash that light at us, she must be able to see that we're doing what she says," he grumbled to Abby as she splashed through a shallow rivulet behind him. "Why does she have to keep—"

Wait a minute. He turned his head toward the lights. Had the patterns of dashes and dots changed? It had.

••• — ——— •—• ••• — ——— •—• ••• — ——— •—•

STOP STOP STOP

"Whoa." Sam stopped walking. Behind him, close enough to touch, Abby did too.

A low growl came at them through a dense thicket of alder bushes, a tone so deep it hummed along Sam's rib cage. Branches and leaves about ten feet ahead of them heaved and shook as something big and brown forced its way through.

A grizzly bear.

CHAPTER TEN

"Don't run," Sam whispered to Abby. He unzipped his jacket and stuffed his hands in the pockets, spreading his arms out wide to make himself look bigger. The bear took a look at him and halted, swinging its head from side to side and snuffling, as if trying to decide what Sam's smell meant. Was he a threat? Was he a meal? Or was he just in the way?

"Let's back off," he said, keeping his voice low. "Maybe if we get away from it . . ."

She didn't answer. Sam didn't dare look away from the bear. He could see the heavy, dense brown fur swinging slightly on the bear's frame; the claws, streaked yellow and brown, on its massive feet; its small, dark eyes. "Abby?" he croaked.

He caught a flash of movement out of the corner of his eye. Abby was gone! She was sprinting toward a tall spruce tree uphill from the riverbank. Sam had time for a moment of astonishment—wasn't it the worst thing you could do, to run from a bear? He'd grown up in a suburb and he knew that! And Abby had lived in the wilderness all her life! She was the one who knew how to handle the mountain lion. What was she *doing*?

Then the bear charged.

It was like watching a huge brown mountain heave itself into motion. How could anything that big move that fast? Without even thinking, Sam was running too. Maybe it was wrong, maybe it was right, but it was the only thing to do. He had to get away!

He tore uphill, his feet digging into slick mud, his hands pawing at rocks to get a grip. How close was the bear? He could hear breath huffing from its nose; he could hear claws on rocks. Any minute—any second—those claws would be in *him*!

The shadow of a pine tree fell over Sam. He looked up and jumped, grabbing a long, horizontal branch that stretched out over his head. He swung and heaved his feet up too, locking them around the branch. Something snagged his backpack and yanked. Desperate, he clung to the branch. Cloth ripped, and he was suddenly lighter. A strap of his backpack had given way and the pack dangled from one shoulder as he hugged the branch, wiggled, twisted, got his weight up onto it, and looked down.

Less than three feet below him, the bear snarled. Sam's heart was pounding so hard, it seemed to bang into his rib cage and send vibrations buzzing down his bones. He'd never known how *big* a grizzly was. The thing looked like a wall of brown, like a tank—not like an animal at all.

Grimly, on hands and knees, Sam inched toward the trunk of the tree. Why did they always put bears in stories for little kids? Had none of those writers ever seen the real thing? Or *smelled* it? A stench of old fish and unwashed fur rose up and choked Sam's nostrils.

He got to the trunk and, clinging to it, climbed carefully to his feet. Below him, the bear seemed to be doing the same thing. Slowly it rose up on its hind legs. No! If that thing stood up to its full height, it could swipe Sam off this branch as easily as he'd swat a fly off a windowsill. Sam grabbed a branch above him and scrambled up. Another branch. Another.

Panting, he looked down. The bear dropped back to all fours and paced around the tree. It didn't seem to want to leave. Sam sat on his branch and hugged the trunk. He could stay up here longer than any bear could stay down there, he figured.

Then the bear rose up on its hind legs again and hugged the tree.

Was it doing this to try to *shake* Sam out of his perch? Were bears that smart? No, it wasn't. Sam stared down, appalled, as the grizzly took a good grip on the trunk with its inch-long claws and awkwardly heaved itself up. The thing was climbing up after him!

Sam scrambled higher into the tree, as the bear came up below him, faster than anything that big should be able to climb. The tree shook under the animal's vast weight, and Sam had to grip hard, his hands stinging from scratches and sticky with pine sap, his arm muscles starting to throb. He was lighter than the bear, so he could go up higher, right? Where the branches were thinner and the animal wouldn't be able to follow him, right?

He had to stop when he reached a branch about as thick as a baseball bat that bent under his feet. The branches above were even skinnier. He was trapped. And the bear was still coming.

Hugging the tree with one arm, Sam reached back into his pack. Bears liked honey, didn't they? Sweet things? Well, maybe he had something that would help. His fingers closed around something sticky in a crackling wrapper— his half-eaten Snickers bar.

Sam aimed carefully and let the candy bar go. It bounced off the bear's nose and fell to the ground.

The bear shook its head, startled, and paused.

"Go on," Sam muttered between clenched teeth. "You want it, right? Candy? Much tastier than me. Go get it!"

Maybe the bear heard him. It craned its head as if wondering where the interesting-smelling projectile had gone, and then began to move again—this time *down* the tree.

All of Sam's joints felt watery with relief. He eased himself down to sit on his thin, creaky branch, gripping the tree's trunk, as the bear scrambled back to the ground, nosed through the pine needles for his Snickers bar, and ate it in one gulp.

"Okay, you've had your snack," Sam told it. "Time to get moving. Don't you have somewhere to go?"

Apparently the bear didn't. It seemed to have no inclination to climb the tree again, but it also didn't seem to want to go anywhere. It scratched through the dirt at the roots of the tree and nosed through drifts of golden pine needles as though hoping another candy bar would appear.

Sam thought of pitching pinecones down at the bear, but maybe that would just make it mad. So he sat. After a while the bear sat too. Then it stretched out with a long, whiffling sigh that Sam could hear all the way up the tree.

Sam groaned.

His butt was beginning to go to sleep. Cautiously he eased himself down to a slightly lower, slightly thicker branch. He sat for a while more. He alternated between looking down at Smoky the very lazy bear and out at the view.

Under other circumstances, it would have been pretty—he could see the river meandering through its valley, a thick rope of gray and white and silver spilling and splashing over smooth, dark stones. He could see the mountains surrounding the valley, steep slopes carpeted in light green, then dark green, then bare rock, then, on the highest peaks, snow. He could see a clearing in the forest not far from the river, where eight trees had grown in a circle. Kind of odd, really. He remembered Abby saying that nothing in the wilderness went in a straight line, not for long. So what in the wilderness grew in a perfect circle?

But never mind about that—where *was* Abby? The bear had followed Sam, so Abby must be okay . . . he thought. But if she was okay, wouldn't she try to find Sam? He strained his eyes, hunting for a trace of Abby's purple jacket down there in all that green, but he didn't see anything.

He did *hear* something, though.

A loud blast on a whistle. Another. The bear stirred and shook its head, as if it didn't like the sound.

Another. The loud shrill noise tearing through the forest. Grumpily, the bear heaved itself to its feet, growled, took a final swipe at the tree with its claws as if to prove a point, and lumbered away between the trees.

Was it gone? Sam eased himself down a few more branches, but not all the way to the ground. He could hear more blasts on the whistle now, and feet tromping through the bushes, and voices calling, "Sam? Sam!"

Marty! And Abby! Sam slithered down a few more branches just as the two girls, with Theo behind them, appeared at the foot of his tree.

"Hi, Sam," Marty called, looking up at him. "Did you decide to build a nest up there?"

"Very funny." Sam climbed down the rest of the way and jumped to the ground, his pack swinging from one shoulder.

"Sam, I'm *so* sorry." Abby's eyes were wide and full of remorse. "I can't believe I took off like that—I just panicked! Then I ran into Marty and Theo, and we headed back to find you."

"You should have had a bear whistle, Sam," Marty told him, waving her bright silver whistle at him. "If you make enough noise, the bears hear you and get out of your way."

"I wouldn't have needed a whistle if you hadn't sent us straight toward the bear!" Sam shot back. "What was that all about, Marty? Telling us to go northeast?"

Marty blinked, startled. "I didn't tell you to do that."

"Sure you did. Do you think I can't read Morse code? You said, 'Bear NE.'"

Marty shook her head. "You thought that meant—? I was trying to *warn* you about the bear! That there was a bear to the northeast!"

Oh. Sam thought for a second. So Marty's message hadn't been "Bear NE"; it had been "Bear! NE!" That did kind of make more sense, now that he thought about it.

"Anyway, never mind." Marty flapped a hand, brushing away Sam's near-mauling experience. "We found the next clue! Theo and I could see it from up on the cliff. There are eight trees near here—"

"Planted in a circle! I saw those!" Sam said.

"I don't think it's a circle. I think it's an octagon!" Marty's eyes were gleaming. "Remember Thomas Jefferson and octagons?"

"Let's go!" Sam said, leading the way. "You know, Marty, since you saw those trees from the cliff, and I saw them from a tree by the river, maybe we were both right about the clue on the tombstone."

Marty, falling into step beside Sam, gave him a quick glance out of the corner of her eye. "Maybe."

Silently, Theo followed them. Abby had dropped several paces to the rear, so she wouldn't have to walk beside Theo. Sam glanced back, thinking maybe he should walk with Abby, but for the moment he decided to stay where he was.

They hiked under trees for perhaps half an hour, finally reaching the clearing Sam had sighted from the top of his tree. They eyed the ring of trees in the center, a circle perhaps fifteen feet across. "Eight of them. Definitely an octagon," Marty said, her eyes narrowed as she thought.

"I wonder who planted them. Maybe it was Josiah!" Abby started toward the ring of trees. The others followed more slowly.

Once inside the circle, Abby paused by a birch tree and looked startled. "Huh. That's weird." A metal plate had been set into a knot on the narrow white trunk, and a long, thin lever stuck out from it.

"Abby, don't—" Marty started to say.

"Not a good idea!" Sam burst out, moving quickly forward.

But before they could warn Abby that, when you were dealing with the Founders, it was best to be careful about pushing buttons or turning handles, she had taken hold of the lever and pulled it.

They heard a loud, grating squeal, as if a rusty hinge was opening, and the ground shook hard beneath their feet.

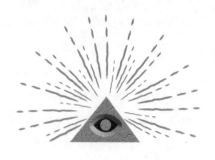

CHAPTER ELEVEN

Sam was thrown on his face in the soft grass, and he heard Abby shriek. He staggered up to see that the birch tree was gone. It had fallen straight into a deep pit that had opened up underneath it, and Abby was clinging to the side of that same pit. She'd grabbed at the grass before she fell, but her grip wasn't enough to hold her weight. Her fingers were slipping slowly through the dirt.

Sam lunged forward. "Don't let go!" he yelled, flinging himself down and grabbing for both of Abby's hands. She gripped him frantically, her fingernails biting into his skin. Sam dug his knees and elbows and feet into the earth, trying to brace himself, but it was no use. He was inching forward, Abby's weight pulling him down with her.

Then Marty thumped on top of him, anchoring him with her weight and knocking the breath out of him, and Theo threw himself onto his knees beside the pit, grabbing Abby beneath her arms.

For a moment Abby's eyes met Theo's, and Sam saw something strange on her face—astonishment? Confusion? Resentment? Then Theo said, "Pull! Now!" and all three of them heaved, dragging Abby up over the edge of the pit.

Marty rolled off Sam. Abby sat up, shaking. "Thanks," she said, her voice wobbling. She glanced at Theo and then away.

Theo didn't say anything—but then, that was typical. "No problem," Sam wheezed. "Geez, Marty, what do you have in that pack, a set of weights?"

"You're welcome," Marty said tartly.

"Yeah, yeah. But, Abby, just so you know—it's better not to, you know, pull on things. Or step on bridges, right, Marty?" Marty snorted. "Or whatever. Old TJ was a typical Founder, all right. He loved making things difficult."

"Well, that's kind of the point," Marty said. "It's *supposed* to be difficult if you don't know what to do. If we had Jefferson's descendant here, we'd know."

"But he's in Nepal, so we're stuck with *difficult*." Sam looked around. "And that's what we've got, all right."

When Abby had pulled that lever, it hadn't merely opened up a pit beneath her feet. A rough circle of ground inside the clearing, with the ring of trees at its center, had dropped down as well. It had been that movement that had tossed Sam on his face. Now they were at the bottom of a hole maybe forty feet across and ten feet deep.

How could the earth just fall down like that? Sam frowned. He yanked up a handful of grass by the roots and poked into the hole he'd created. Under about three inches of dirt was a rough metal surface. The entire clearing was a fake.

"I bet there's a crater below us, or a sinkhole," Marty said. "And the Founders built this on top."

"But trees can't grow in just a few inches of soil!" Abby said, puzzled.

"I don't think they did." Sam got up cautiously, in case the ground beneath his feet planned to do any more gymnastics. It stayed steady, however, and he approached the octagon of trees, except that now, without the birch tree in it, it was—what had Marty called it?—a heptagon.

Sam reached out to tap an oak tree, and nodded. "Fake. Metal. I bet they all are."

Marty was at his side. "So they were made. Not planted."

"Right." Cautiously, staying on the outside of the circle of trees, Sam moved on to a maple. "And they all have those metal plates, look. With handles."

"And if we pull the wrong handle—" Marty glanced at the pit where the birch tree had been standing and shuddered. Sam could not see a bottom to the hole where, not long ago, Abby had been dangling.

He nodded. "So let's not do that, okay?"

Theo spoke up. "We don't want to pull the wrong handle. So which one's the right one?"

"There has to be a way to figure it out." Sam continued his prowl around the ring of trees. "It's a puzzle. It has an answer." He had to give the Founders that much. They were happy to kill anybody who got a puzzle wrong . . . but they did give you at least one chance to get it right.

"All the trees are different," Marty said.

"So?" Sam answered. "Trees are probably like snowflakes. No two the same."

"Different species, I mean. The one that fell in was a birch. Oak, maple, elm, cherry . . ." Marty paused. "The cherry tree. Remember George Washington, cutting down the cherry tree?"

Theo shook his head. 'That's a myth. He never really did that."

"And this isn't Washington's puzzle anyway," Sam put in. "It's Thomas Jefferson's. What kind of a tree would TJ have?"

Marty looked blank. "I can't think of anything . . . wait! Virginia!"

It was Sam's turn to look blank. "There's a kind of tree named Virginia?"

"No, Sam. The state tree of Virginia. Jefferson was from Virginia." Marty closed her eyes, thinking hard. "I know this . . . Give me a minute . . ."

"Does she really know that?" Abby whispered to Sam, awe in her voice. "The state tree? Of every state?"

"I bet she does," Sam answered, keeping his voice low as well to let Marty think.

"Flowering dogwood!" Marty announced, opening her eyes and grinning. "I remember because it's the state flower too."

Sam grinned too. "Marty, you're amazing. Which one's flowering dogwood?"

Marty turned in circle, gazing at the trees. "It's . . . it's . . ." Her grin faded. "It's not here."

"You're kidding." Sam felt his shoulders slump. "I was sure that was right. Thomas Jefferson, Virginia . . ."

"You told me sometimes you have to guess wrong the first time to guess right the second." Marty's face took on a look of fresh determination. "So the state tree isn't the right answer. Something else about trees and Jefferson, then—oh. Oh!"

"Marty! What?" Sam demanded.

"I am so stupid. I can't believe I didn't see it before!"

"Marty! Just tell us!"

"The elm tree! The tree of liberty!" Marty practically shouted.

"The tree of what now?"

"Honestly, Sam, anybody would think you'd never read a book. The Liberty Tree, on the Boston Common! The colonists gathered there to protest the Stamp Act! It was a huge symbol of the resistance."

Sam nodded. "And it was an elm tree, I'm guessing?"

"Give me your backpack!"

"Huh?" Marty snatched the pack from Sam's shoulders as he twisted around to stare at her in astonishment. "Marty, chill. Yes, I've got another Kit Kat in there. You could have just asked."

"You've got Josiah in here!" Marty pulled out the urn with the ashes of Abby's ancestor. "Don't you remember what was carved on this? Thomas Jefferson said it! 'The tree of liberty must be refreshed from time to time with the blood of patriots and tyrants!'"

"Okay, okay! Marty, we're convinced. The elm tree is the tree of liberty. Fine. Do the honors." Sam nodded at the elm.

"But what if . . ." Abby's voice trailed off. "Be careful, Marty. What if you're wrong?"

"Nah." Sam grinned. "Marty's always right, Abby. It's in her name. You get used to it."

Marty snorted. With Josiah's ashes still in her hand, she stepped up to the elm tree, found the metal plate, reached up, and pulled the lever.

Sam braced himself, but the ground did not move. No pits opened up. No earthquakes shook their surroundings. The metal plate on the elm swung meekly open and inside was another. This one had a circular hole in its center, its edges notched like rough saw blade, with a pattern of triangles.

Marty looked down at the urn and up at Sam. He nodded.

"Looks like a keyhole to me, Marty. Try it."

Marty did so, tipping the urn sideways and sliding the top, with its jagged, saw-toothed edge, into the hole. She frowned, hesitated, and twisted the urn. There was a click. The top of the urn had opened.

"The blood of patriots," Marty said softly, as Josiah's ashes fell from the opened urn into the tree's hollow center.

Then there was a crunch.

Sam jumped forward, ready to grab Marty if she started to slide away into a bottomless pit, but that was not what had happened. A small section of the clearing inside the ring, perhaps four feet square, had slid open, revealing a set of stairs leading downward.

"So we go down," Sam said, and headed for the staircase. The others followed.

The stairs were wrought iron, curving in a spiral. Sam went down cautiously, alert for more Founder tricks, but nothing happened. At the bottom of the staircase, he found himself standing in the center of an octagonal vault. The walls were white granite, polished to a gleaming shine. On one wall, engraved in silver and as tall as Sam's head, was a pyramid with an eye atop it and a quill in its center.

In front of this engraving was a simple wooden desk, worn by time. On it stood an inkwell, and beside the inkwell was a quill.

Not an ordinary quill, though. This one was silver, as bright as though it had just been polished. Sam hesitated and glanced back at the others.

Abby looked wide-eyed and anxious, hugging her arms across her chest. "I—I don't like closed-in places," she said suddenly. "I'm just going to—wait outside. Okay?" Before anyone could answer, she had dashed up the stairs.

That was kind of weird, Sam thought. For somebody with claustrophobia, Abby had seemed fine the whole time they'd been in the cave behind the waterfall. But he didn't want to spend too much time thinking about that now, because he was about six inches away from . . .

"Go ahead, Sam," Marty said. "You're closest. Pick it up."

Sam reached out a hand for Thomas Jefferson's Quill.

"This is it, huh?" He turned it gently in his hands. "The real thing."

Theo spoke up. "It's real."

Sam had held a Founders' artifact once before, but at the time there had been a very scary guy with a gun in the room, and Sam's attention had been divided between holding Benjamin Franklin's key and not dying. This time there was nothing to take his mind away from what was in his hands.

The Quill Thomas Jefferson had used to write the Declaration of Independence.

Someone—Thomas Jefferson himself?—must have taken the Quill and dipped it in molten silver. Every little curve and delicate tendril of the feather it had once been had been perfectly preserved. It seemed familiar, somehow, as well. Was it just that Sam had seen a thousand pictures of quill pens like this in history textbooks, in movies, in books?

All men are created equal.

Thomas Jefferson had written that with this pen. What Theo had said about the man was true. He'd owned slaves. He'd kept his own children as slaves. And it had probably never occurred to Jefferson that women—like the ones Marty and Abby would grow up to be—would like to be considered equal too.

But he'd written it. He'd thought of it. Old TJ had said to the world: We don't *have* to have some sort of system with royalty on the top and the rest of us spread out at the bottom. Instead, we can start out by thinking that we're all the same. That a pawn can be as powerful as a king.

Maybe there hadn't been perfect equality in this country when Thomas Jefferson had written that, Sam thought. Maybe there still wasn't perfect equality today either. But it had been a start . . . and it had started with this Quill.

Theo let out a slow breath, interrupting Sam's thoughts. "That was . . . simple."

Sam blinked and looked around. "I know. I was expecting the ceiling to fall on our heads, or something. I guess old TJ figured that if we made it this far, we were the real thing?"

"I guess so." Marty looked amazed and relieved too. "Come on. Let's get it out into the light. I have an idea . . ." She headed for the stairs as well. "Abby, look at this!" she said, once they had all reached the surface. "Do you recognize it?"

Abby had been standing with her back to the staircase, facing out through the ring of trees. She turned and frowned. "Recognize what?"

"The Quill. Sam, show her!" Sam held the Quill out so Abby could see it. "It's just like the quill in the polygraph back at your ranch," Marty told her, and Sam nodded. *That was why the Quill had seemed familiar!*

"There were supposed to be two quills in that machine," he said. "I bet if we put this Quill in beside the other one, it'll tell us what we need to know!"

"What we need to know?" Abby looked confused.

"Where the next artifact is!"

Marty nodded, her eyes shining. "You're right. I'm sure you're right, Sam. Ben Franklin's key told us to come here . . . and the Quill will tell us where to go next. We just have to get back there quickly!"

"Quickly," said Theo, "is going to be the tricky part."

"Well, we just . . . we just . . ." Sam's voice trailed off. He looked around. They were at the bottom of a ten-foot pit, created when the cover over the crater had dropped down. First they had to get out of that. Then they had to . . . what? Find their way back to the abandoned town, follow the ancient road, clamber through the cave system (and hope the mountain lion wouldn't be lurking around), climb *up* a waterfall, follow a river, and finally hike back to Caractacus Ranch?

It would take *days*, Sam realized. Could they even do it? They wouldn't have horses to ride or rafts to paddle. Would their supplies hold out?

"We'll just get started, I guess," he said glumly.

"It might not be as hard as you think," Abby said. "Look there."

She pointed. A pine tree, maybe twenty feet tall, had been uprooted when the crater's cover had dropped down. Now its roots rested on the edge of the pit, and its crown, in a snarl of branches and pine needles, lay not far from their feet.

"As good as a staircase," Abby said, starting off toward the fallen tree. Sam was a little surprised by how cheerful she seemed. Wasn't she going to argue more with Theo about trading the Quill for her parents' safety? Sam looked down at the Quill, still in his hands. And if she did that, what side would he take?

But an argument didn't seem to be on Abby's mind. She circled the tree and found a way to the trunk through the clutter of broken and bent branches, and she began to climb. The tree wobbled under her weight, but it didn't fall. Marty went next, inching her way upward cautiously, and then Theo. Once the big guy had clawed his way through the massive spread of roots sticking up into the sky, Sam started up.

It was trickier for him, because he was still holding the Quill in his right hand. He didn't want to stuff the precious artifact in his backpack; it would be awkward to explain to Theo or Marty or Evangeline that he had broken it.

Except he wasn't likely to see Evangeline again, was he? Any more than Abby was likely to see her parents again.

Sam didn't like that thought. He shoved his way up through thick branches, his hands sticky with sap, breathing in the Christmasy smell of fresh pine. Theo had made sure they couldn't contact Arnold to hand over the Quill, but surely that didn't mean they just had to give up on

Evangeline. Or Abby's parents, or Theo's mom. There must be *something* they could do.

Granted, Sam couldn't think of what that something might be, but that didn't mean it didn't exist. They'd discovered two of the Founders' artifacts, hadn't they? If the four of them worked together, couldn't they pull off a rescue too?

His foot slipped off a branch, bringing Sam's mind back to his climbing. He grabbed at a muddy root with his left hand, pulling himself up, but he couldn't find a foothold. A hand appeared through the roots, and Abby's voice called out, "Hand me the Quill, Sam! You need your hands for climbing!"

Sam did so, and then, with both hands free to hold on, clambered half over and half through the upturned mass of roots. He fell or slid or sort of both down the other side and to solid ground again. Theo offered a hand and pulled him to his feet.

"Okay, now which way?" Sam asked, looking around. Theo frowned, and said something in return that Sam could not hear.

He couldn't hear it because a deep *thump-thump-thump* noise was growing steadily louder. Helicopters! Sam saw Marty's eyes go wide, saw Abby turn her face to the sky, saw Theo's gaze moving quickly back and forth as he searched for a way out. Then shadows fell over them, and

Sam saw the black machines hovering overhead like giant flying spiders, blocking the light.

They did not look like Park Service helicopters, Sam realized in dismay.

"We should run!" he shouted to Theo, but Theo shook his head.

"Nowhere to go!" Theo yelled back.

And there wasn't. The helicopters were coming down already, generating winds that pounded at Sam, whipping his hair into his eyes, tossing dust and dead leaves and pine needles in a whirlwind. All four kids hunched over and shielded their eyes as the helicopters landed and the disturbed air died down into quietness once again.

Marty moved close to Sam's side as two men stepped out of each helicopter's door. Sam had seen men like this before, in Death Valley and at Caractacus Ranch—large men with large muscles, black jackets, and hard eyes. One of them had a pair of black eyes and slightly swollen nose, probably because somebody had punched him in the face a day and a half ago.

That man moved aside to let another off the helicopter, and Sam's heart sank a little further. Flintlock stepped down to the ground, looking a little too big for his dark suit, his brown hair slightly rumpled, a frown on his craggy face.

Sam shook his head a little, feeling stunned and sick. They'd solved the puzzles, they'd survived the dangers, they'd found the Quill—and now their triumph was about to be snatched away. How did Flintlock find them? How could he have gotten here so quickly?

But the sight of the man who followed Flintlock out of the helicopter drove those questions out of Sam's head. His smooth white suit fit him perfectly; his light hair was slicked back, not a strand out of place.

Sam would have muttered the worst curse he knew, but his mouth was too dry for words.

Gideon Arnold had arrived. Sam knew this was the man who had tortured Evangeline's father to death. He'd kidnapped Evangeline and Abby's parents. And what was he about to do now?

Arnold slid off a pair of sunglasses to study the children with pale-blue eyes. When his gaze landed on Abby and what she held in her hand, he smiled.

Two more people were getting off the other helicopter. Sam turned his head to see them and felt his jaw drop.

Charley and Anita Hodge? Really?

Sam stared, his mind spinning. The Hodges looked good. They had on fresh clothes; they looked rested and comfortable and like they'd had a shower and a fine breakfast before jumping aboard a helicopter for a scenic ride.

They didn't look at all like people who had been prisoners of Gideon Arnold for two days.

And they were . . . smiling. Smiling? All of a sudden, Sam felt very queasy. This was wrong. Nobody should be smiling right now except the bad guys. And that meant . . .

"Dad!" Abby shouted with joy.

She raced across the clearing, Quill in hand, to throw herself into the arms of Gideon Arnold.

CHAPTER TWELVE

Just as he'd been two days ago, Sam was in a helicopter, soaring over the forested valleys and majestic peaks of Glacier National Park.

Well, not *just* as he'd been two days ago. For one thing, Evangeline was not here. For another, this time there were men with guns aboard, and Sam, Marty, and Theo were their prisoners.

And of course, Abby was here this time, sitting on a seat across from Sam, with her father's arm around her shoulders.

Nobody could talk over the noise of the helicopter blades, which was probably a good thing. Sam didn't need to hear any more of Abby's bragging. Down on the ground, she'd pulled a second satellite phone out of a pocket in her jacket. "A lot of good it did you, smashing that other phone," she'd told Theo, a taunting grin on her face. "Dad's been getting regular updates. As soon as I saw the Quill, I told him to get moving. I knew he'd be here in minutes."

Sam, next to Theo, had seen his fists clench and the muscles in his shoulders swell and tighten, and he could tell that Theo was holding himself back from strangling Abby there and then—no matter what Gideon Arnold would do to him afterward. Sam knew how he felt.

It was starting to sink in, just how stupid they had all been. Arnold had known that Sam, his friends, and Evangeline would end up at Caractacus Ranch. Gideon had found the real Hodges three days ago, and he had done everything within his power to get them to tell him how to find Jefferson's key. But when that didn't work, Arnold came up with another plan. Figuring that the Founders would end up at the ranch he installed "Charley" and "Anita," along with Abby, to take their place. They learned everything they could about the ranch in order to make themselves believable as the real Hodges. It had all been an act—their eager welcome of Evangeline and the kids, Flintlock's attack, Abby's terror and grief. It had been a staged show, and they'd fallen for it.

And nobody had fallen as hard as Sam.

He'd *liked* Abby. He'd trusted her. He'd felt sorry for her! He'd listened to her telling him that Theo wasn't trustworthy, that Marty was being brainwashed. And he'd been an idiot all along.

Sam slid another sideways glance at Abby—was that even her real name?—the preteen criminal mastermind he had thought of, half an hour ago, as a friend. She caught his eye and smirked.

Why, why, *why*, Sam wondered, slumping back in his seat, couldn't he meet anyone his age who was *normal?*

It didn't seem to take any time at all before they were hovering over Caractacus Ranch. The helicopters touched down on a flat patch of ground near the barn, and Sam was shoved out of the door by a grumpy man with a gun and a bandage on the back of his head. This had to be the one Sam had knocked into the wall the last time they'd met. The guy kept a fist clenched in the shoulder of Sam's jacket, and Sam didn't have a good feeling about their future acquaintance.

Theo and Marty were pushed out of the helicopter after Sam. "Take them to the dining room," Gideon Arnold said, stepping down onto the ground with Abby behind him. He stroked the silver Quill tenderly and looked over Sam and Marty with cool interest. "We need to test out a theory that my daughter has mentioned to me."

Sam stood his ground, even as the man behind him tightened his grip on his jacket. "Where's Evangeline?" he demanded.

Arnold laughed. "You know perfectly well I have no intention of answering that. I will say that we have a special place for people of distinguished lineage, such as your friend Ms. Temple." That icy-blue gaze moved to Theo. "It seems that our collection grows every day." He strode toward the ranch, and Sam, pushed by the thug with the grip on his shoulder, followed. Theo and Marty were shepherded along behind him.

Our collection grows every day? Sam thought, feeling cold inside. Had Arnold been talking about Theo as the latest addition to his "collection"? Or had he meant Theo's mother?

In a few minutes they were back inside the dining room of Caractacus Ranch. The silver candlesticks lay on the floor where Theo had thrown them; the musket that Marty had threatened their attackers with had been tossed on the table. Those tricks weren't going to work this time, Sam thought gloomily. Not that they had really worked last time. Flintlock's goons had *let* them get to the safe room; they'd only put up enough of a fight to fool Sam, Theo, and Marty into thinking that the whole attack was real.

This time, nothing of the sort was going to happen. Sam's captor let him go, but stood close behind him with his hand (Sam glanced nervously around to see) on the butt of a gun holstered under his arm. Theo and Marty were similarly closely guarded. The three of them had escaped from Gideon Arnold once before, and apparently he wasn't about to take the chance of that happening again.

Flintlock walked in with three backpacks—two full ones, belonging to Marty and Sam, and one flat, empty one, which had belonged to Theo's mother. "Anything in those?" asked Gideon Arnold.

Flintlock pawed through the packs. "Nothing," he said. "Wilderness supplies. Candy bars." He snorted. "This one's empty." He shook the pack that had belonged to Theo's mother and tossed all three to the floor. Sam glanced at Theo, only to see his eyes locked on Arnold, his face wiped clean of any expression at all.

"Very well, then." Gideon Arnold turned his attention to the sideboard under the windows, and the complicated contraption of hinges and levers that stood on it, holding an ancient, tattered quill pen.

"That's the polygraph, Dad." Abby sounded like a teacher's pet, keen to impress. She pointed at Sam. "*He* said we ought to put the silver quill in there, and it'll give us the next clue."

"Let's try it, then." With one stride, Arnold reached the polygraph. He took a sheet of clean paper out of the inside pocket of his suit jacket, unfolded it, smoothed it, and slid it underneath the quill that was already perched in the machine.

"Ink," Abby said. Arnold nodded. He plucked the existing quill from the machine, unscrewed the top of the inkpot that sat beside it, dipped the pen into it, and returned it to its place in the polygraph. Then he dipped the silver pen in the ink as well, and carefully set it into place beside the first.

Nothing happened for a moment, and Sam's stomach twisted into a knot that went all the way up to his esophagus. If his idea worked, Gideon Arnold would know where to find the next Founders' artifact. That would be bad. If his idea *didn't* work, Gideon Arnold would be upset with Sam. That could be worse.

Then both the original quill and the new silver one shivered. With a squeal of old gears and a *scratch-scratching* noise, they both began to write. Dismayed, Sam stared at the quills, wagging as they shaped letters on the paper beneath. He'd been right—he couldn't help but be pleased about that. But his correct guess meant that that they were placing another Founders' artifact into Gideon Arnold's hands.

The quills stopped writing. Arnold delicately slid the paper out from the machine. Sam found he was holding his breath.

"Honor Below Trinity," Arnold read out loud slowly. He looked up from the paper and his gaze landed on Marty and Sam.

"The two of you deciphered Benjamin Franklin's clue and found your way here," he said. "I suggest you do the same now. Get started."

Sam looked sideways at Marty. He knew what Theo would say—that there was no way they should tell Gideon Arnold a thing. But if they didn't cooperate, he was pretty sure they'd be joining Evangeline in Arnold's "special place"—and that was the best scenario. The worst . . . Sam felt a shudder crawl down his spine.

Besides, he had no idea what "Honor Below Trinity" meant.

"The Trinity?" Marty asked. "Well, it could have a religious meaning, of course. Don't you think so, Sam?"

Marty, who'd told him back at the church that Theo was right, that the Founders' artifacts should be kept safe no matter whose lives were in danger? Marty was . . . solving the puzzle?

"Uh . . . Marty . . . I don't know . . . ," Sam said awkwardly, trying to catch her eye. But she was craning her neck to see the piece of paper in Gideon Arnold's hand, and she seemed to be in pure puzzle-solving mode. Sometimes Marty got so wrapped up in being smart she forgot to be anything else—like, say, aware that she was helping out the worst bad guy on the planet.

"But I don't think it's a religious reference," Marty went on, as if she hadn't noticed Sam's reluctance. "It could be . . . of course! Trinity College, in Connecticut. That's it, I'm sure that's it. It wasn't around in Revolutionary War times, but it was definitely there by the Civil War, and that's when all the artifacts were moved. The next artifact must be hidden somewhere in Trinity College!"

"My, aren't you useful." Gideon Arnold folded his piece of paper and tucked it back into his pocket. Marty stood with her mouth slightly open, dismay dawning on her face, as if she had just realized what she had done.

"Way to go, Marty," Sam muttered. She didn't have to hand the clue to Gideon Arnold on a silver platter, after all. Sheesh. At least the three of them could have endured a little torture before selling out their country.

"It might be beneficial to keep these three around for a while," Arnold said, eyeing them with a greedy light in his eye. "But for now, put them in the barn with the others. We'll need a little time to make travel arrangements."

"The barn" turned out to be an outbuilding stacked with hay, not too far from the stable where Sam had first made the acquaintance of Snickers. He caught a glimpse of the black mare in the corral, chewing moodily on a wisp of hay. Her ears swiveled forward and she whinnied at the sight of Sam as he was hustled past and shoved into the barn. Theo and Marty followed close behind.

"The others" turned out to be Charley and Anita Hodge—the *real* Charley and Anita Hodge. At least, that's who Sam assumed the two adults were. They had been tied, back to back, to one of the support beams that held up the roof, and securely gagged. Had they been there three days now? Sam thought, appalled. All the time he and the others had spent at the ranch, eating hamburgers and sleeping in comfortable beds—all the time they'd spent searching for clues in the wilderness—these two had been here?

Both were slumped forward against their bonds. The woman turned her head slowly to look at Sam, Theo, and Marty as they were pushed inside, her eyes dull. Her brown hair, streaked with gray, hung loose about her face. The man didn't stir.

Sam hadn't needed any more proof that Gideon Arnold was a ruthless man . . . but now he had it. The men who'd brought them here pushed all three kids to the floor. Flintlock followed them in and dumped their packs on the ground. He stood watching as one of his men stood guard with a gun while two more made quick work of tying up two more prisoners. Sam and Theo were tied like the Hodges, sitting back to back against one of the support beams. Painfully tight ropes held their hands to the sides of the beams, and more ropes were fastened around their chests. Marty was lashed to a beam by herself.

Flintlock nodded in approval and jerked his head toward the door. The men left without a word. Sam heard a lock click as the door slammed shut.

Sam squirmed, trying to get a good look at the building. It was small, maybe twelve feet square, and stacked with rectangular bundles of hay. Snickers's nightmare, he thought to himself. A barn full of hay and no candy in sight.

Pretty soon a barn full of hay was going to be Sam's nightmare too. He'd bet on it.

Sam twisted to the other side, trying to get a better look at the woman tied up behind him. "Hey, are you Anita? Anita Hodge?" She didn't answer. Her head had fallen forward once more.

"They're not in good shape. Dehydration can be very serious," Marty said, sounding worried.

"So can being tied up by a homicidal maniac." Sam tried to work his hands free but only succeeded in shredding his wrists. "We have to get out of here!"

"I think we've all grasped that, Sam." Marty was squirming in her bonds too, bending her knees to draw her feet closer to her body. "Theo, can you . . . ?"

Theo lunged forward against the ropes, straining to break free. Unfortunately, all this accomplished was to yank the ropes around Sam's chest even tighter. "Theo! Stop!" he choked out as his rib cage neared implosion. "I can't— *ouch*—breathe!"

"Sorry." Theo panted, slumping back against the pillar. "That didn't loosen anything up, did it?"

"No! It really didn't." Sam's ribs throbbed. "Brute strength isn't going to do it. Marty, don't you have, you know, anything? A knife? A flare? A secret decoder ring?"

"Sure. In my pack. All except the stupid ring thing." Marty cast a longing glance at her backpack, sitting near the door, as out of reach as if it were on Mars. "All I've got is some matches in my boot. You know, just in case."

"Matches?" Sam perked up. "Matches are good. Can you get to them?" Any other time a snarky comment might have made its way out of his mouth—only Marty would think to tuck matches inside her boot! But right now it seemed perfectly reasonable to Sam. If they got out of this alive, he was going to start carrying all sorts of things in his shoes.

Marty had her knees drawn up to her chest by now, and was trying, grunting and grimacing, to pull her feet close to her hands, tied behind her. "I can't . . . I can't do it," she gasped.

"Don't give up," Sam said.

"I'm not giving up, Sam!" Marty had changed tactics. Using the heel of her right foot, she was energetically trying to shove her left boot off her foot. "It's—*ouch!*—tight. I think I can get it off, though." She pushed, winced, tried again, and the boot popped off. A book of matches fell out onto the straw-covered floor.

"Way to go, Marty!" Sam said, this time for real.

Marty wiggled around and kicked the matches toward Sam and Theo. Her aim was good. The book of matches landed close to Theo's right hand, tied inches from Sam's left. "I'm not going to be able to strike one with my hands like this," she said. "What about you guys? Can you work together?"

Theo, straining to pick up the matches, pulled hard at the ropes again, nearly dislocating Sam's shoulder blade. "Careful!" he gasped.

"I am . . . being . . . careful!" Theo had his hand on the book of matches now, and leaned back against the beam, giving Sam some relief. "Why are you so short, anyway?"

"Why are *you* built like a yeti?" Sam asked. He could feel Theo's right hand, near his own left, working at the book of matches. "Don't drop it, whatever you do." Sam groped and felt the smooth cardboard of the match-book cover. "Okay, I can hold it still. See if you can pull a match off."

Theo did and promptly dropped the unlit match to the floor.

Sam groaned. "Marty, how many matches are in here?"

"I think three," Marty said.

Sam groaned again. *"Careful,* Theo."

"I heard you the first time you said that, Sam," Theo said. Sam heard the faintest possible ripping sound. "Got a match. Hold the matchbook still. *Still . . ."*

"That's what I'm doing!" Sam tried his best to concentrate on the feel of the matchbook. He could feel the slick, smooth cardboard of the cover and the sandpaper-rough surface where a match was meant to be struck. Then he felt the match's head rubbing on that surface. "Yeah, Theo, that's right. Right there. Go!"

"First-degree burns are mainly superficial," Marty told them helpfully.

Theo pulled the match as quickly across the rough surface as he could manage. Nothing happened.

He did it again.

Nothing happened again—at least, that's what Sam thought at first. Then he felt heat against his fingers. "Yes! You did it! Theo, you're the man—ouch! *Ouch!"*

"Hold your hand still!"

"Burn the rope, not my hand!"

"Even second-degree burns can be treated!" Marty called out. "They very rarely result in permanent scarring or limb amputation!"

"Okay! I think the rope's burning! Sam, do you think so?" Theo asked.

"I think *something's* burning!" Sam couldn't tell at the moment if the rope or his sleeve was on fire, but he was sure that something was. "Pull! Theo, pull!"

Theo strained against the ropes again, forcing all the air from Sam's lungs. Sam couldn't even yell as sharp pain jabbed at his left hand and wrist. Then suddenly the ropes gave way, and Sam's left hand was free.

It was also on fire. His sleeve was blazing merrily away. Sam slapped his arm against his chest to smother the flames, and twisted and writhed to get free of the rest of the ropes. Theo was doing the same.

Sam yanked his right wrist free and turned to slap Theo on the back. "Theo, you did it! Didn't I say you were the man!"

Then he yelled and scuttled on hands and knees toward the barn's door. The burning ropes that had tied Sam and Theo to the beam had fallen into a patch of hay close to where Sam had been sitting, and the fire had already started to spread. A stack of bales along the wall farthest from the door was alight.

Sam stared in horror. *Out of the frying pan, into the fire . . .*

CHAPTER THIRTEEN

Hay burns fast, Sam discovered. Really, really fast. The
flames swarmed eagerly up the bales of hay and reached
into the loft overhead.

"Sam, get the door!" Theo yelled, already coughing.
He was untying Marty, while Sam raced to the door, his
eyes starting to sting from the smoke, sweat breaking out all
over his body. Sam wrenched at the doorknob and kicked
at the door. It shook on its hinges but didn't open. The
lock was solid and strong.

Marty joined him, hopping as she shoved her hiking boot back on her foot. She also threw her weight
against the door, with no effect. A few seconds later,
Theo reached them as well. He had untied the Hodges
from their beams. Anita, stumbling and staggering, had

roused enough to help him drag her husband's limp body across the floor.

"Is there another way out?" Sam demanded.

She shook her head. "Only the hayloft," she croaked, her voice faint. Four pairs of eyes lifted up to the blazing loft and then back down to the door.

"Theo, get us out of here!" Sam said. Theo slammed his shoulder into the door. It bounced in its frame. He kicked at it. One board splintered.

"Yes!" Blinking hard, his eyes watering, Sam took turns with Theo, kicking at the broken board. They managed to knock the board out of the door, but the gap it left was narrow, about the width of Sam's arm. No way they could squeeze through it.

Theo attacked the next board, but Sam fell back, coughing. This wasn't going to work. They wouldn't break the door down in time. Maybe the hayloft after all? No. One look was enough to convince him of that. The loft was a wall of flames, and the smoke was so thick that Sam could no longer see the ceiling.

There had to be another way out!

But maybe there wasn't. This wasn't a computer game or a crossword or a Founders' puzzle. Those were guaranteed to have an answer, if you could find it. This was a burning building with a locked door. Even if you were smart like Marty, or strong like Theo, or a puzzle master like Sam, there might not be an escape route waiting to be found.

One of the planks from the roof fell with a crash into the hayloft and toppled over the edge, bringing a fresh blaze of heat with it. Sam felt the hairs on the back of his neck start to fry. In a few minutes the floor would be burning. They were trapped. They couldn't get out.

No. No way. Sam closed his stinging eyes for half a second. When you couldn't think of an answer—when a puzzle had you stumped—it meant you didn't have the right approach. You had to change the way you were thinking. You had to come at it a different way.

They couldn't get out of this barn . . . but maybe somebody could get in?

"Theo, move!" Sam choked out. He pushed Theo aside and shoved his face against the gap in the door. Desperately, he squeezed a high, loud whistle out of his parched mouth.

Theo's hand fell on his shoulder. "Sam? What are you doing?"

"Disorientation is a sign of carbon monoxide poisoning!" Marty shouted over the roar of the flames.

"Snickers!" Sam gasped. "Here, Snickers!"

"Sam! Have you lost your mind? Get away from there!" Theo pulled at his shoulder again. "Maybe I can . . ."

"No, Theo. Let him do it!" Marty got her words out just before a fit of coughing doubled her over.

"You little sugar-loving maniac, come on!" Sam called as loudly as he could manage. Then an idea flashed into his head. He grabbed his backpack, lying on the floor next to his feet, and ripped it open, dumping the contents out on the floor. Raincoat, broken flashlight, water bottle—there! He snatched a bag of marshmallows and seized a handful, soft and sticky from the heat. He'd been thinking of a marshmallow roast when he'd stuffed them into his pack—a bonfire in the night, toasty brown treats on sticks. He just hadn't imagined himself being *inside* the bonfire.

Sam thrust his handful of marshmallows out of the gap in the door. "Candy!" he yelled. "Come and get it!"

A few seconds later, a damp, furry nose nuzzled at Sam's palm. He let Snickers have a marshmallow, and then pulled his hand back inside.

"C'mon, Snickers," he muttered. "More! More! You want more, don't you, Snickers?"

Snickers's nose disappeared, leaving the gap in the doorway empty.

"Oh, Sam," Marty said. "It was a good idea anyway . . . What are you doing?"

Sam was backing away from the door, stamping on flames under his boots.

"Getting out the way," Sam told her. "You do it too." Theo bent, took a quick look through the gap in the door, and flinched back.

"Everybody move!" he yelled.

Marty jumped to one side. Theo helped Anita Hodge drag Charley's body to the other. And Snickers slammed through the door, breaking its planks as if they were toothpicks, heading straight for Sam and the marshmallows in his hands.

Five humans and one horse tumbled out of the broken door two seconds later. The humans coughed and slapped at sparks in their clothes and hair as they staggered to a safe distance from the fire. The horse whinnied impatiently and stuck her nose in Sam's face until he fed her handfuls of marshmallows from the remains of the bag. "You earned them, girl. Good Snickers," Sam told her, patting her as she ate.

Charley Hodge, stretched out on the ground, began to stir and cough. Anita, kneeling beside him, stared up at the three kids in wonder. Marty handed her a bottle of water from her pack. "Drink it slowly," she said.

"Who are you children?" Anita asked, her voice weak. "I don't know . . . what's happening . . ."

"Later," Theo warned, bending down to heave Charley Hodge to his feet. "We've got to get out of here before anybody up at the house sees the fire."

Marty tossed Sam's pack at him; she had snagged her own and the one belonging to Theo's mother as she raced out the door. "The stable. We can get horses," she said. "Looks like Sam already has one of his own."

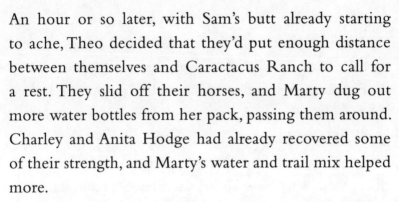

An hour or so later, with Sam's butt already starting to ache, Theo decided that they'd put enough distance between themselves and Caractacus Ranch to call for a rest. They slid off their horses, and Marty dug out more water bottles from her pack, passing them around. Charley and Anita Hodge had already recovered some of their strength, and Marty's water and trail mix helped more.

"I was sure we were going to die in that barn," Anita said softly from her seat on a moss-covered fallen log. "Those men stormed in when we were at dinner three nights ago and grabbed us."

"We know what they wanted," Charley said, swallowing half of the contents of the water bottle at one gulp. "The question is, did they get it?"

"The Quill," Theo said with a sigh. "Yes, they did."

Charley Hodge eyed him. "You know about . . . that?"

In a gesture that took Sam back to a time two days ago, Theo rolled up his sleeve, revealing the tattoo on his arm. Charley Hodge's eyes grew wide. "You're a Founder?"

Theo nodded. "And now we have to make a plan," he said.

"To get to New York," Marty added.

Sam, leaning against Snickers's side and sharing a roll of SweeTARTS with her, shook his head. "How are we going to get anywhere? We've got no money. No car. We can't just buy plane tickets."

"We can," Theo said. "Evangeline made sure I knew what to do, how to get to the Founders' money if I needed to." He swallowed. "She wanted to make sure I could . . . go on. If something happened to her."

"Oh." Sam nodded. "So we can get to New York after all . . . Wait. Why New York?" He swiveled around to stare at Marty. "You told Arnold the next artifact would be in Connecticut!"

"Alexander Hamilton is buried in the graveyard of Trinity Church in Manhattan," Marty said, as if this explained everything.

Sam stared at her. "So?" he asked.

Marty sighed. "So Alexander Hamilton was killed in a duel with Aaron Burr, who was Thomas Jefferson's vice president. A duel, Sam. Meeting on the field of honor? So *Honor Under Trinity* must mean Alexander Hamilton's grave at Trinity Church." She looked at Sam's wide-eyed expression and put her nose up in the air. "Well, it's not like I was going to give Gideon Arnold the *real* answer," she told him.

A slow grin spread over Sam's face. Marty could drive you crazy, with her facts and her guidebooks and her constant chatter. But if you needed somebody on your side in a crisis, there was nobody better than Martina Always-Wright.

"We can help," Charley Hodge said. He leaned against a tree trunk, his face exhausted but his eyes determined. "I'm sworn to help the Founders any way I can."

"*We're* sworn," Anita said, reaching to take Charley's hand. "And even if we weren't, we'd help. After what you've done for us."

"Okay!" Sam fed Snickers the last SweeTART. "Then we'll do it." He felt his confidence returning, rising up through him. They weren't alone after all, the three of them, and they never had been. Even when things had been at their worst—when a mountain lion had stalked them through a cave, when they'd been inches from burning to death, when someone who'd acted like a friend had turned into a traitor—the three of them hadn't been alone, because they'd always had each other.

So maybe Marty was a know-it-all who talked too much. So maybe Theo had his secrets, and he and Sam didn't always think the same way about the Founders and the artifacts and how to protect the world from the likes of Gideon Arnold. And the two of them might be thinking right now, *So maybe Sam's kind of a slacker and he's never serious and his jokes aren't even all that funny.*

But the three of them could trust each other. Sam realized that he knew that, deep down, without question. He didn't have to wonder if Theo or Marty would suddenly turn out to be like Abby, a liar or a traitor, working for the bad guys. They had their flaws—so did he—but they were on the same side.

He remembered standing among the pieces of the giant chess game, surrounded by kings and bishops and knights, with his hand on the pawn that would win the game. Because the important thing about chess wasn't how powerful you were. It was all about where you were standing, and who was standing with you.

Sam spoke up. "We'll find Hamilton's grave." *Somehow*, he thought. "Theo, we'll find Evangeline too. And your mom." *Somewhere.*

Gideon Arnold had said it: "We have a special place for people of distinguished lineage." *A special place* meant Evangeline and maybe even Theo's mom weren't dead. They were being kept somewhere—somewhere they could be found.

It was a lot to do, and there'd be no one to show them the way. From now on, they'd be making their own decisions. It would be up to them.

"I don't know." Marty looked over at Sam, and he could see the worry in her eyes. "The next artifact . . . Evangeline . . . Theo's mom . . . how are we going to find all of that on our own?"

Theo was staring off into the trees, and for the first time Sam could remember, the big guy looked just a little helpless. Like he didn't know exactly which way to turn.

"The same way we've done everything else so far," Sam told his friends. "Together."

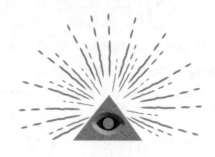

POSTSCRIPT

Dear Mom and Dad,

Guess who's been exploring Glacier National Park in Montana!
We really got off the beaten path. I got to try river rafting
and horseback riding, and even got a close-up look at some
of the wildlife. The Lewis and Clark Expedition passed close
by here, you know—Thomas Jefferson sent them to find out
all they could about our country. I'm finding out a lot too,
especially about how important good friends really are.

Sam